The Resurrection of Jesus

A Novel

By

Yancey Williams

ISBN: 978-0-9860316-9-4 (Paperback)
ISBN: 978-0-9860316-4-9 (Ebook)

The Library of Congress has catalogued the YPress edition as follows:

Names: Williams, Yancey, author.
Title: The Resurrection of Jesus: a novel/ Yancey Williams
Fiction/Satire | Fiction/ Suspense.

Published in the United States by YPress.

To Bill Devereaux
All-Around Rodeo Champion
Indian Rodeo Hall of Fame
Montana Indian Athletic Hall of Fame
Itákkaa. Aissksinima'tstohki. Friend & Teacher.

He lives, He lives, Christ Jesus lives today!
He walks with me, and He talks with me,
Along life's narrow way.
He lives, He lives, salvation to impart!
You ask me how I know he lives:
He lives within my heart.

Alfred Ackley

CONTENTS

Chapter 1 Further on Up the Road..1

Chapter 2 Aamsskaapipikani—Blackfeet Nation 5

Chapter 3 Aamsskaapipikani II—Blackfeet Nation II........................9

Chapter 4 Aamsskaapipikani III—Blackfeet Nation III 12

Chapter 5 Aamsskaapipikani IV—Blackfeet Nation IV 16

Chapter 6 Aamsskaapipikani V—Blackfeet Nation V......................18

Chapter 7 The Prison Diary of Jesús Ángel Escobar 24

Chapter 8 Ksistsikam Ayikinaan—A Voice from Nowhere 32

Chapter 9 The Painting in The Trunk of the Car..............................36

Chapter 10 Coming Full Circle—The Vatican Loaner in a
            Three-part Switcheroo..39

Chapter 11 D'Artagnan du Vitet—Of Pride, Prejudice,
            & Happenstance...43

Chapter 12 The Tables Turned..46

Chapter 13 Jesus Sketches 54

Chapter 14 Jesus Saves! 59

Chapter 15 Aamsskaapipikani VI—Blackfeet Nation VI.................62

Chapter 16 When Jesus Went to Prison—Cuando Jesús
Fue a la Cárcel..66

Chapter 17 The Spirits in Prison 79

Chapter 18 The Crucifixion of Jesus By Jesús Ángel Escobar........83

Chapter 19 The Third Cell Down on The Right...............................85

Chapter 20 Naatowá'pínaa—Holy Man from the Cave of Hira.....88

Chapter 21 The Fatwa & Hobby Goes to Jail 90

Chapter 21 Payback Under the Elm—Venganza Bajo El Olmo...102

Chapter 22 Jesus Calls Back..107

Chapter 23 Aamsskaapipikani VII—Blackfeet Nation VII............110

Chapter 24 Witten Kingsland?...117

Chapter 25 A'póóhsin Aakáítapissko—Trip to the Big City.........120

Chapter 26 Shawnee Mae Meskwaki & The Vatican Loaner.........122

Chapter 27 Nipápao'kaanistsi—In My Dreams 129

Chapter 28 Áókaki'tsi—Scouting Ahead 139

Chapter 29 Stand Up at the Comedy Lair Featuring
Hobby Alif Ali-Ali..142

Chapter 30 Eighty-One Minutes At Isabella Stewart's Garden.....149

Chapter 31 A Day Late...153

Chapter 32 Mohsokó ni Otomohk—The End of the Road............159

CHAPTER 1

Further on Up the Road

It stood out. The *Jesus Saves* part. The big, bold letters on the side of a weathered, tattered and frayed, dilapidated, old billboard.

The message read,

The Devil was on my back.

He was heavy and riding me hard. But, not no more cause I found Jesus.

Below that pitch, a bearded Jesus appeared in cameo. Sandals, arms outstretched, hands healed and open. His robe fit prophetically, tony for the times. It was the sympathetic Jesus all wrapped in forgiveness, the one with the quiet, pensive persona. Right there He was on the front of the big sign, Jesus, the real deal. He'd risen, just like the Bible and the board said He would.

Beneath that was the bigger question.

Is the Devil on your back, too? Is he heavy and riding you hard?

Just Remember, my friend. Jesus Saves. Jesus Saves. Jesus Saves! *And, He can save you, too.*

Framed in a forty-by-sixty-foot crimson, pinewood border, the monstrosity was in the middle of nowhere. By its sheer size, you would have thought that the sign would be speaking to a much larger audience, but not so. *Nowhere* was a broad field deeper than it was wide, plainly measured between other open fields and long stretches of tattered barbed wire most of which was distressed, grounded, and loose ended, set some distance from a grove of leafless willow trees and scrub oak. The support timbers leaned in separate directions almost like poorly concocted decoration, perhaps interpretative, surely suggestive, even metaphorical, a tangential and bucolic bust of sorts but only if you used your imagination.

Neon lime green lettering embroidered in bloody Golgotha skull and crossbones, the whole thing was encased in imitation hieroglyphics and knock-off Hebrew Sanskrit. It was twice wrapped in clusters of body tattoos sporting toothy gargoyles, a cascade of catholic angels complete with open wings, and a frightened, devil-red Satan fleeing. It was a mighty fortress, and a mighty fortress is our God. It said so in the right-hand corner in a starched, tight font. It was quite noticeable. You couldn't miss it. Not if you were on the way into town on Jackson Highway.

Ten miles down the road just south of the giant sign, Jesus Escobar stood on the outside of a tall prison gate that had just closed behind him. He struck a match against his trouser leg. He cupped his hands and lit the cigarette between his teeth. He blew smoke into the wind with a workmanlike sigh. For the first time in a long time, he was a free man.

Ten miles the other direction, two guys sat in different sedans parked side by side behind the *Jesus Saves* monolith in short underbrush. They watched from an abandoned service road that was now merely a swath of its former self between the throes of kudzu and leftover bramble. From a distance, the two men surveyed the highway out front. There was a clear view just underneath the heel of Jesus' left sandal and the Jekyll-like gargoyle grinning and positioned in that same corner. The sign board obscured their stakeout. They counted cars waiting for the right match.

Back down the road the other way, Jesus Escobar stood vacantly inside his faint cloud of cigarette smoke. It was a vapory residue.

His smoke rings just as quickly blew away. Six unfiltered Camels in a few unnoticed minutes, one right after another after another. He was roadside. He stood there and mumbled to himself in Spanish. *Gringo.* He said it out loud, *Gringo,* like there's someone around to hear him. It was inconsequential. It was just Jesus Escobar and Jesus roadside alone.

Someone inside told him there would be cash in his pocket and a car waiting for him just outside the prison gate for the ride downtown, but it was bull shit. There was nothing. He suspected as much before he got to the curb. Prison was bull shit, too.

There was a playlist of songs spinning round in his head. There was no particular reason. Reason be damned. It just was. Mariachi melody after mariachi melody, one to the next. Verse to chorus. Chorus to verse. The whole thing stumbled from one misbegotten norteño phrase to another, then to a body of lapsed lyrics. Trumpets and open vihuelas in a cancion ranchera beat. The melody carried on even when he turned to view the road beyond where he stood.

A car passed. Then another. He fumbled about in his trouser pocket and pulled out a small flip phone, the one he'd just stolen off the desk of a prison guard in the waning seconds before his release. He dialed ten numbers, pushed send, and pressed the receiver to his ear. He waited. Then, he turned half way again away from the wind.

"Yo," said Escobar. There was a lilt in his voice. "Quick, it's me, Jesus." He listened. He smiled. "Cómo estás? Yeah, kemosahbee, you thought I was dead, but hell no, bro, I've risen. I'm out. Risen like Jesus his self, mo fo. This Jesus has risen, too. Come down off of the cross, Quick, and I'm as free as a bird. Libre. Libre como un pájaro, Quick."

A cold, fast west wind came in off his left shoulder. There was a vibrato inside every gust. It cut through to his skin. It would have hollowed his spirit, but he found comfort and life in his conversation. Escobar turned his back to the forward side.

A dark sedan pulled over in a sudden stop and the driver inside yelled, "Get in." Then said, "No, in the back," from behind the side glass. The driver pointed with a long thumb to the back seat. The driver, un hombre negro, wore a black beret.

Jesus Escobar said, "Quick, I'll call you back. Just got a ride into town. Más."

CHAPTER 2

Aamsskaapipikani
Blackfeet Nation

My name is Hiram Johnny Walker Quicksilver. I (Niisto) am Blackfeet. Siksiká. Niitsitapi. A rightful tribal member of the Blackfoot Confederacy and Asmsskáápipikani. I am a proud warrior. So, too, was my grandfather. So, too, was his father before him.

I am Hiram to my mother. I am Quick to some others.

I own four cowboy hats, five pair of cowboy boots __ three pair are worn plum out__ and a pair of silver and gold spurs. I won the spurs in a dogging event at an Indian rodeo fifteen, sixteen years ago. Long time I know, but who's counting? The rowels they glitter when they spin. Beautiful to see. I feel like Gary Cooper when I put them on and walk full stride across hardwood.

I own one silver bracelet the width of tired latigo. The silver bracelet, it is a sentimental piece. It is capped with four turquoise nuggets each one nearly the size of a baby calf's testicle. Also, I own three saddles, a breastplate made of carved and polished buffalo bone, and a headdress so full of eagle feathers it hangs to the back of my brown bowlegs. The headdress, it was my grandfather's. It was the headdress of my grandfather's father before him. It is only for Indian ceremony and sacred celebration though I will *admit that I did get married in it. It made me feel very proud. It made me feel very, very important, too, like I owned the universe and all the stars in the big sky.*

That was when I married Esther from Las Vegas ... Las Vegas, New Mexico. Esther, she was Pawnee. Esther, she was a proud woman. She walked forever with her shoulders back, her head up, her chin out, and her eyes wide. A cantilevered delight and tits to back it up.

Esther, most of the time, she drives me crazy, me, Hiram Johnny Walker Quicksilver. Fucking crazy, and, yes, those are my best words exactly. I say those words (fucking crazy) so many times I lost count. She disagrees just to disagree. She agrees, somehow, to disagree. The woman throws tantrums and shit across the room. She said it allowed her to express herself and make her point. Okay, okay, I guess. Point made, Esther from Las Vegas, New Mexico. Tantrum to another tantrum. These tantrums, they were like twin bucking bulls spinning out from an open chute; couldn't tell them apart. Then, threw twice as much shit to make the same point again. Said it was to drive it home, like I didn't get it the first time. I got it, woman. But, this is Esther, Esther from Las Vegas, New Mexico, the Pawnee. Tantrum or no, it was the woman that I, Hiram Johnny Walker Quicksilver, married. You know, for better or worse.

Whoa, Esther, I would say. Whoa, Esther, whoa. No reins long or strong enough to hold her. Esther, she was all woman and a Pawnee to boot. She was from Las Vegas, New Mexico. I know, I said that already three times. But, that's okay, she was.

Sure, Esther, she loved to flirt with me on her good nights. She teased me best at every new daybreak rubbing everything she had up against me in every way she could think, and me half asleep. That feeling, me and her lying there twisted and contorted and gathered together, I know it is what paradise and heaven must be in the afterlife if there is one.

But she flirted, too, with other Indian braves, the ones who she knew would make me maddest. Younger ones, half my age. She liked the younger ones. This is what she said for everyone to hear, me included. Smiled and cooed and batted her big brown eyes. Her eyes, they were as wide as a barn owl's, tender as a new fawn's. Braided her hair just so for the barroom, the slow dances, and romantic bedtime. Mister Quicksilver, that is what she would say. Romantic bedtime, it was my favorite. Called me Chief Quicksilver on special nights when we'd been drinking open shots of Canadian whiskey. Again, Esther drove me crazy, but lots of times it was really good, a good crazy and worth the ride if you know what I mean.

"Worth the ride ... if you know what I mean" ... sure, I'm messing with you. You know what I mean.

Great Indian sex, how to describe it? Two kindred spirits, warriors of the flesh. Feathers fly. Whooping. Hollerin'. Tomahawk chop. Battle cries into the night. Hokahey! Hokahey! Everything less the war bonnets and face paint. Scalping of sorts, you might say, but with better and heartier purpose. Hard for an Indian to really sweat per se, just not in the red man's DNA (Don't Never Ask what I call it.), but not during sex with Esther. Two bodies drenched in Indian sweat like a couple of cutting horses at a noon day summer branding. I always say this ... Indian sex what first made the aspen quake.

It makes me grin to tell that joke. Not my best joke, but still a good one.

Esther, she is my squaw, Hiram's squaw for sure. Quick's aakíí. But, Esther demands equal rights, so to speak. Squaw is ahead of her time, an Indian women's libber, you know ... so to speak. (Hiram Johnny Walker Quicksilver, the Blackfoot warrior and rodeo rider, I say so to speak because it makes me sound smart ... so to speak. Indian living in the white man's world ... so to speak. Just messing with you again ... so to speak. Cursed, but got to go with the flow ... so to speak.)

Here again, me, Hiram, I always smile in the telling.

But the equal rights thing. No, not like that, not what you think. Equal rights was to Esther half on top, half on bottom. Sex and ride 'em cowboy equal rights. That was Esther's line, "ride 'em cowboy".

"Equal rights", that was mine. It was fantasy made real. On this, we both agreed. No argument there.

Esther, she had tits the size of Whitehead torpedoes. (Torpedoes: My time as USMC private first class to corporal in eight months. I was a good soldier.) But back to Esther. Hers were even more shapely, brown as saddle leather and firm to the touch, but even better than that. The Great Spirit smiled when Esther made love to Hiram Johnny Walker Quicksilver ... when Esther sat atop his war eagle.

That's a good one, you have to admit, "sat atop his war eagle" not like some of the other Hiram Johnny Walker Quicksilver one liners that are limp and stale or maybe past their prime.

For the record, Esther, she was on top when Jesus called.

CHAPTER 3

Aamsskaapipikani II
Blackfeet Nation II

*B*est cowboy ever?
That's what I say. I say it real loud over everything going on. Everybody at the bar gets real quiet. Don't say nothing. Everybody at the bar looks back at me, Hiram Johnny Walker Quicksilver. They know I know my cowboys.

Then, I say, "Casey Tibbs?" Then, I wait for a second or two. Then, I say, "Or, Larry Mahan?"

I paused between the two cowboys' names just because I thought it was the right thing to do, show some respect. A lotta broncs between the two.

That's how it started. Just like that. I emptied my pockets (sure I'd been drinking) and put it all on top of the bar, right smack dab in the beer foam and whiskey overflow. Dollar bills, fifty cent pieces, quarters, three silver dollars, a buffalo head nickel, four pennies, one dime, and a rabbit's foot attached to my truck key.

I say, "Casey Tibbs," just like that but louder. No one says nothing. I wait. Too drunk to answer I guess, so I wait some more. I rummage into my watch pocket. I find another crumpled five-dollar bill and slam it onto the bar with the flat of my palm, beer foam flying.

The entire bar is silent. Everybody is looking around at everybody else. They're thinking. I can tell. They keep thinking. Best cowboy ever? They keep thinking some more. Casey Tibbs or Larry Mahan? It's a tough one so I take another shot of Canadian whiskey while they mull it over. Remember, it's late. We been drinking since sundown, probably before. It's snowing outside. What the hell better than snowing and drinking (besides sex with Esther).

I'm feeling the buzz. Grinning a lot. Hat pulled down next to my eyebrows where I like to wear it when I'm drinking. Let's me concentrate better on the horizon and the pretty girls. My ears are sticking out from the hat being pulled down so low. My saddle bronc rider look. My doggin' look. Lets me hear better in all the bar racket ... the jukebox, chatter and laughter, the billiard balls clacking against one another over in the corner. Some country & western crooner is singing something in the backdrop.

A half a dozen bar stools down, Red Snake pipes up.

"Larry Mahan," he says. He tips his hat.

I look him over and shake my head. A put up or shut up shake my head look.

Red Snake was the new Indian. Native American, he called it.

Red Snake couldn't ride a stick horse out of a mud puddle, but he was all Indian. My fault, Native American. Wore his hair in a woman's braid with silver bracelets and turquoise necklaces on his hairless chest. Soft hands ready for nail polish. That night he wore pigtails under his Tom Mix ten-gallon Stetson. Jeans tucked in at the pull strap of his rose-colored boots, the ones with the long stovepipe, embroidered shaft and fancy Cuban heels. He was a movie star. Never been on a bronc. Never been in a movie. On his good days, he fixed lanyards and beaded trinkets and bitched about his rights and the white man this and that.

"How you figure Larry Mahan?" I said.

"Cause I never heard of Casey Tibbs," said Red Snake.

When I hit Red Snake, I knew I wasn't as drunk as I thought I was. It felt good. My fist was balled up perfect-like. When I get it right, my fist looks like the iron end of a sledge and close to the same size. Red Snake, his face splattered like a ripe pumpkin over a cedar fence post. That's when I knew I was in trouble.

Then, Red Snake, he fell quicker than a Douglas fir inside a clap of thunder. His head hit the floor, his boots ricocheted off one another, and three women gasped for breath to get a better view.

"He's dead," one said.

"Ah, hell, he ain't dead," I said. "He's just knocked out." I showed her my clenched fist as proof. I poured a whiskey in his face, ice and all, one from off the bar, but Red Snake he never budged.

He was *dead.*

Sheriff and two deputies came in through the front door. They carted me off out the back, then across the alley to the squad car all lit up like a Christmas tree. Pushed my head and handcuffs into the caged backseat and away we went. Prison wasn't no fun, but that's how I got there, and that's where I found Jesus. He was on the top bunk just down the hall, talking to himself in a mix of Mexican and petty English with that smirk on his face like he'd just killed another Mexican.

Come to think of it, he had.

Me and Jesus, we wasn't no art thiefs. We didn't know Picasso's palette from a bucket of house paint ... or Jimmy Six Killer's doggin' horse, a gelding. He was a paint. Good horse. Take you straight to the steer. No curves, no hitches, bobbles, or balks. Never shied away from them horns or got distracted in all the hoofs pounding and the arena dirt splashing up around your face. Hazers loved him, too. Good horse. But, like I say, me and Jesus, we wasn't no art thiefs. But, we learned quick enough.

CHAPTER 4

Aamsskaapipikani III
Blackfeet Nation III

When I (me, Hiram Johnny Walker Quicksilver) got out of prison, I did okay. I got religion real fast. It seemed the right thing to do. Plus, it made people less afraid of me. (Me, you know, a convict. Killed a man. People talk.) For starters, I spoke in tongues for nine days straight at the Pentecostal church. That's how I found my niche. I became something of a local celebrity. Everyone came to watch. I was entertaining for sure. They said, "You should see Hiram Johnny Walker Quicksilver. He's back. Out of jail, preaching, and speaking in tongues over at the Pentecostal church." I admit I liked it. And, the pastor loved me. He didn't have to say nothing because I was so convincing and did most of the talking for him. Sometimes I'd shake all over, sometimes I'd stomp and stamp and gyrate, but I was always saying something no matter what. Got everybody riled up and filled with the spirit. The crowd put lots of money in the offering plate, and, then, me and the regular preacher, we split the take at the end of each meeting.

The pulpit tribal cadence was more like a drunken dialogue between me, Hiram Johnny Walker Quicksilver, and God, the Almighty, the big man in charge. At least that's the way I sold it. What's more, after a few services and then a few more, I began translating religious talk *and made-up scripture into aboriginal Blackfeet. It was mostly psycho babble and war chants. Mostly, I say. A little Siksiká here and there, but I would run out of stuff to say in any language the prayer meetings went on so long. I did this for the better part of ten or twelve months until one night after a double meeting (money was real good on two-a-days), I got so dizzy I fell down a flight of stairs. I knocked myself out cold. Woke up later hungover with a knot the size of a door knob on the front of my forehead. Hurt like hell for days. Some people spread the rumor that God had spoken to me, was punishing me, said I should quit, I was making a spectacle of myself, but that wasn't it at all. God didn't say nothing. We never spoke. Anyway. After the fall, that's when I gave up preaching. The money was good, but I'd had enough. Didn't have nothing left to say. That's the reason I quit. Honest Injun. (A little more Quicksilver humor for you.)*

My late cousin he owned a Russell. He said it was a painting of a cowboy holding the reins to his sorrel, overlooking an open ravine. Two Indians on horseback in the distance. Cowboy doesn't see them. Probably sunset or real close. There was a big sky, no clouds. Anyway, it was a Russell. This was a long time ago. C.M. gave it to his grandfather. They were friends, C.M. and the grandfather. Swapped horses and livestock. Something like that. Anyway, the painting burned up when the house caught fire. That far out, say sixty, seventy yards from the river, no chance. House went up like a matchstick, saddles, blankets, tables, chairs, a sofa, three nightstands, C.M.'s painting, everything. Nothing had no chance. Cousin got out alive, but he was lucky. That was it. Started all over from scratch. I know the feeling.

Anyway.

That's all I ever knew about art. Russell had his museum and the stuff in it was supposed to be worth a lot of money. That's all I know now.

So, as for the art thing, someone (never knew who and never asked) pointed us in the right direction, and we figured it out from there. Like I said, I started all over.

So, anyway.

Where was I?

When Jesus called back, he tells me how the man that gave him a ride into town kept running off at the mouth. Said the man was insulting him, calling him names, jailbird, pipsqueak, wetback, spic this, spic that. Swore he heard him say pissant. The man sort of mumbled when he talked. Maybe some kind of an accent. This according to Jesus. Asked him if in prison he ever took it up the ass. Then, asked him (guess this threw him over the edge) if he ever sucked a cock and did he like it? Then, Jesus said he sees this picture wire in the backseat on the floorboard, picks it up, coils it around his one fist three or four times, then coils the other end around his other fist three or four times, and loops it over the man's head deep into his throatlatch. About that time, I protested, but it didn't do no good.

I said, "Jesus, you just got out of prison, bro'."

"Sí, sí," he says, "but the dude pissed me off."

He said the car came to a stop in a slow roll while the man was kicking out the front windshield with his new Florsheims trying to get away. Jesus ain't real big, but he's strong for a little fellow not to mention feisty and crazy as a barefoot, moonstruck Comanche straddling an open cactus patch. So, anyway, the car dies weaving about in the middle of the two-lane back road, Jesus crawls over the dead man, puts the car in park, and drags the dead man to the back so he can put him in the trunk. "Santa mierda," *that's what Jesus says to me on the phone to which I said,* "Holy shit what?" *To which Jesus says,* "I go to put the dude in the trunk and there's this picture or picture frame rolled up in an old army blanket. When I uncover the frame, there's this painting lying there. It was like nothing I ever seen."

I'm listening. Jesus keeps talking.

"Quick, I know nothing (nada) about this stuff, pinturas or artwork, but this one jumped out (saltó) off the canvas at me. It was different, high quality. The thing could almost talk. (Casi podría hablar.) You know how sometimes you can just tell even when you know you don't know nothing. Well, I could tell, and I don't know nothing. I'm telling you, it's worth some money. Aquí. Here, on the back, Quick, the dude autographed it. Rembrandt somebody, or somebody Rembrandt. Es famoso, Quick? And look here, says, La Resurrección de Jesús, The Resurrection of Jesus at the top. Hey, Quick, qué coincidencia, they named it after me." (The crazy little Mexican, he laughed out loud.) "Something, ain't it? Fantástico. Huh, Quick. Jesus Escobar finding the painting of the real Jesus in the car trunk of un hombre muerto."

Jesus said he picked it up carefully, had it wrapped up like a newborn, then took it and set it down gently in the back seat so it wouldn't get knocked around. Even locked the door like it was gonna jump up and run off or something. Said he went back and lifted the dead man over the bumper and rolled him into the trunk, Florsheims and all. Said the dress shoes wasn't his size, or he'd've swapped 'em out. Just like a Mexican. Indians, we don't do that. Ain't taking shoes off a dead man. Might kill him, but he can keep his shoes.

Scalping's a whole nother matter altogether. (A little Quick humor, again.)

I'm listening to Jesus real careful when I hear him let out an "Oh, shit," but it wasn't too loud. He'd sorta dropped the phone from the side of his head. I could tell something wasn't right. He says, "Somebody's shooting at me, Quick. Just blew out the side view mirror." I could hear the car door slam and the engine crank, then Jesus says, "Quick, got to go. Luego te llama. I'll call you later, recluso. Más." Then, he hung up.

I knew somehow, we was in business.

CHAPTER 5

Aamsskaapipikani IV
Blackfeet Nation IV

I t was the third time Jesus called.

Esther handed me the phone on the dismount. She said, "It's for you."

We was going good. A lot of rhapsodic hollering and filthy dirty talk in between the mashed flesh. Ohkaania'si! We had to stop before climax the phone rang so many times.

"Damn," I said.

Then, I answered like I was out back scaling trout for a late breakfast.

"Hey, Jesus, my man." (Hiram talking.) "Long time no see. Where you at, bro?"

"E Z money."

That's what Jesus said to me. Then, there was a pause.

"E Z money."

He said it the same way the second time, just like he'd said it the first. Exactly the same way.

He doesn't say, 'Hey, this is Jesus,' or, 'Guess who?', or 'Cómo estás?' Nothing. Just, "E Z money."

"Big job," he said.

"Fast, too," he said.

"Just like that," he said. I could hear him snap his fingers like he always did when he called the guards on duty (Prisa, prisa!). Can't see it. We're talking on the phone, but, I know him. He always snaps his fingers, like that, snap, when he sees something happening quick like. So, I could see him. Probably holding a cigarette between his teeth and smiling.

"Big job," he said. "And no problema for you and me. Piece of cake'. Swoosh and abracadabra. Like that. In and out. We're done." Jesus, he said, "It will take two maybe three hours the whole thing. We pack our shit, and we're gone. Cabo. Hawaii. Tahiti, maybe. Never been. Nunca ha sido. You, amigo?" Jesus blew smoke rings, smiled and asked, "You?" He takes another hit off his cigarette and said "Wherever your big, dumb Injun ass wants to go, we make so much money on this one you can go. You hear me, Quick? Me oyes, Quick, you there?"

I said, "Yeah, yeah, Jesus, I hear you, kemosahbee, I hear you loud and clear. We make so much money, me and you, we end up back in the can?"

I laughed like hell, out loud, Esther lying there, her face puckered up like what you two ex cons dreaming up now to get in trouble? Esther with her big tits laid out for all the world, with her arms behind her head waiting to ride 'em cowboy again. She's always patient.

"Naw, hombre," said Jesus. "No way, Jose. Confía en mí. It's a piece of cake, Quick. Trust me, kemosahbee. You'll see."

I told Jesus Escobar, "We have to talk more about all of this. You and me. Just you and me."

Me, Hiram Johnny Walker Quicksilver, I like to talk out fables and mysteries and folklore in a life that makes no sense. Yes, you could say that. Quote me if you like. Tell 'em that's what Hiram says.

CHAPTER 6

Aamsskaapipikani V
Blackfeet Nation V

Many times I talk to God. Aatsimoyihkaan. You know, me ... the Indian praying ... so to speak.

Hold on one second, said Hiram.

Let me, Hiram Johnny Walker Quicksilver, sit up straight in the chair. I have to get out the rodeo kinks. It lets me think better. The words they become more clear and easier to translate, Siksiká to white man's point of view.

There. Now, that's better. It frees up my hands so I can express myself that way as well. An Indian thing you might say.

(Hiram leaned in and continued.)

Anyway.

I should say, many times I try to talk to God. Not the white man's prayer, but the Indian's way of speaking to the Great Spirit. Aatsimoyihkaan, it is the Blackfeet way.

Not the same thing, again, but you get it. Try ... ssanisttsi in Blackfeet ... here is the key word.

I spoke out loud on every occasion. No one was conducting an interview (like I was a famous person or something), but I spoke out into the open air like there was someone, maybe God himself, the

Great Spirit, Á'pistotooki, there asking questions and waiting for my reply. At the same time, I always curl my thumb over an old wound on my index finger. The wound, it reminded me always to be humble. A roping wound. Saddle horn, rope, then index finger where it didn't belong. Rope stretched out with a steer on the end of it. Finger wasn't supposed to be there; not in the manual. (Hiram smiled.) *But, my finger, it was still attached. Fast thinking I always say.* (Hiram smiled.)

If I'd been thinking fast, wouldn't've happened, right? (Again, Hiram smiled.) *Okay. You're keeping pace. This is good.*

My finger never healed right. Crooked. Cut to the bone. Flesh hanging, bleeding all down my pant leg onto my boot. Hurt like hell, but it healed up pretty good for not doing nothing to it.

Anyway.

He, you know God (pointed to the ceiling), *never answered. One voice, mine, filling the space around me. One-way conversation. One person in the room ... me. Gets old. Man in a pinch is better off dialing nine one one. At least somebody picks up the receiver, and you hear someone say "Hello", or, "nine one one", or, "how can I help you", or something. A voice recording is better than nothing. Even if they don't get there in time at least you got to talk to somebody before you die. You call, sometimes you get put on hold you know, but that's okay because you know they're coming back on the line to see what you're calling about and how big's your problem. You know ... send the ambulance or send the hearse or send the empty fuckin' horse trailer, for Custer's sake. At least you know something's coming for you. Praying, it didn't get me shit. A room full of nothing and empty all bundled into one. No bailing twine neither.*

Yeah, I know. Just my opinion and me talking. Sure. But it's what I know happened to me. Hey, speak for yourself. All I got in this life is what's happened to me. I ain't no Geronimo. I ain't no Abraham Lincoln. No Cochise. Just me, Hiram Johnny Walker Quicksilver. Blackfoot Indian. Piegan warrior. Barroom brawler. Team roper. Bulldogger. Bronc rider. Steer buster. Tie down in under nine and half seconds every time, maybe faster on a good day, but consistent. Calf don't stand a chance. Okay. Then, say, under ten seconds no questions asked. All in one. Feather in my cap and two good fists to bust you with if you cross me.

With God, never got no answer. Tried to talk to Him. You know, in private, like you're supposed to. Reverent, respectful, quiet, humble like. I did that. It's God.

Horseback once, some place in the aspens trailing three elk, two cows and a bull. Ponoká. Big ones for sure. I was alone. Nothing except me and my roping horse breathing heavy and farting sometimes to break the silence. No God that I could tell.

Beneath the pickup more than once, too, tried to talk to God. But, one time I remember looking up at a broken tie rod thinking where the hell I'm going to get the money to fix this. So, I said, Hey, God, where the hell am I going to get the money to fix this? Huh? Huh? I said huh twice. Not a peep. Just me sweating and cussing from the grease and dirt falling off the undercarriage into my eyes. All I got out of that was a black band of sludge across my brow when I wiped the sweat off with the back of my shirt sleeve. No God.

Out in the woods, figured it had to be the place to talk to God. Walking slow and quiet, you know, the Indian in me, beside my horse. Saw the biggest buck I ever saw. Rack as wide as the grill on my truck. Figured it was an act of God for sure until I looked down into an empty scabbard. It was tied crossways to the front of my saddle, but I had left my rifle on the bed next to a box of shells and my bedroom moccasins. Outdoors, seemed like the best place to talk to God, but, again, I got nothing.

This is funny. Not just another Hiram Johnny Walker Quicksilver joke either. I know you will like this one. Indian talking here.

Tried smoke signals once just for the heck of it. Mary Two Feathers said to me her cousin sent smoke signals to God from the back side of Chief Mountain (Nínaiistáko). Got what he wanted in three days. That's what Mary said. I said, "Damn." Mary wasn't a bullshitter. (If

I didn't have Esther, I would chase after Mary.) So, anyway, figured it can't hurt. Tried burning brush and dry leaves, wet saddle blanket over a dying campfire, green branches over old timber, hell, I tried it all. Smoke everywhere. You could see the gray fog coming out of the treetops clear over on the Nez Perce reservation two hundred miles away. Still nothing and no God.

You know Smokey Bear would show up before God. Too bad I guess. I say talking to God is harder than picking a lottery winner with a Canadian fifty cent piece.

Saved the best for last and the last one. Promise. Bear with me.

Dialed a fake number once. Spelled out H-e-a-v-e-n. One eight hundred heaven. Nothing. Not enough numbers. Maybe too many. Don't know. Never even got a busy signal. Nothing. Not a voicemail. Not even a dial tone. Nothing. You know, you dial out a few times and talk into the receiver and nothing happens you just quit calling that number. Waste of time. Phone's disconnected. Somebody forgot to pay the bill. Just like an Indian not to pay the fuckin' bill. Anyway. Either He ain't listenin', He ain't home, or He don't care and ain't got the time to fool with me. Either way, figure I'm screwed. Hey, so what's new? Make the best of it and move on. Little fellow, this Indian (points to his chest with his nubby, thick index finger), *left out in the cold again.*

Make no mistake. I didn't just try to talk to God. I listened, too.

That voice that's there inside your head, that inner voice, all crystal clear and shiny, always giving you orders and directions on which way to go and what to do, the same one that's supposed to say God loves you, you know like when you're in a bind ... I never heard that ... not in my life. I heard people say that to me... God loves you, Hiram Johnny Walker Quicksilver, He does, and then I'd think to myself, well, if He does, He's got a funny way of showing it. But, I never did say nothing back to them, and I never heard nothing even after they said that. Personally, for me, it was a bust and a wash. But again, it wasn't like I wasn't listening ... I was. Or, being disrespectful... I wasn't. Nothing or nobody ever talked to me from out of the sky or the trees or from behind a wall at least nothing I could ever recognize or translate. Not in Blackfeet. Custer's English neither.

I was always waiting, listening. And still am. But still, I got nothing.

No bush rustling, twigs snapping, snares with a catch rope, no cloud formation spelling out 'Hey, Hiram Johnny Walker Quicksilver, over here. It's me, God' ... no buffalo grass catching fire and crawling up my pant leg to get my attention ... or a badger (always pissed off) coming up out of his prairie hole squawking Siksiká (God-like) telling me 'do this or do that or don't do this or don't do that'... nothing either from the clear sky or the dark sky or from behind the quaking aspen. I been listening the whole time. Hey, God, where you at? says Hiram.

Maybe God, He's on one of those frequencies you know like a dog hearing the high-pitched sound of a whistle you can't hear. So what chance have I got of hearing God? I never heard nothing at a dog's pitch. Again, not in the DNA, kemosahbee. So, maybe only the white man hears Him ... God, you know, and in some secret code. Maybe the Big Man, He's a telegraph operator. USMC (me), but not a telegraph operator. Left up to the Navajos I suppose. Maybe they talk to God. Know a few. I might ask.

Television preachers, they all say they talk to God, hear God, get directions from God, moved in with God, took a wrong turn without God ... the same television preachers always wanting money. So, get a loan from God, dude, says Hiram Johnny Walker Quicksilver. And while you're at it, get me one, too. Need a new pickup ... bad.

Ain't got no money, pulpit boy. I'm an Indian brave. A Warrior. A Rodeo rider. Those three and money never did go together.

(And Esther's stallion, too. Don't want to leave that out, but still no money.)

Anyway.

Jesus said show up. So, I did. Talk to the man he said. So, I did. Twice. Cell connection was good. The man (name, City Chief), he said we would make us a lot of money. More money than I ever seen. That's what he said to me. More money than a man will need or can spend in this lifetime.

This man, boss man (Chief for short, Nínaa to the Blackfeet tribal warrior), City Chief, he said he was part Cherokee, a quarter Tsalagi. But that's what they all say when they're talking to a real Indian. Every white man east of the Mississippi is part Cherokee particularly when they need to be because they want something. City Chief (saw a picture of him), he had dark hair and a scar on his left cheekbone, but that don't make you Indian. Can't ever remember his last name ... Cochise-something or Crooked Bear or Crawling Fox or Clawing Horse ... whatever ... can't recall. Nice enough fellow I guess with the beautiful girlfriend (she was in the same picture), legs up to here and a waist no bigger than the honda knot on my tie-down lariat. Jesus said she was a nun before now. Hard to believe that though. No nun I ever seen looked like that. Don't believe it as a matter of fact. There was too much edge to her ... a strand of barbed wire in a field of spring clover. No nonsense. She was the blunt end and the razor's edge of an axe blade in one. All business. I mean Boss, he was all business, but she made him look like he was playing stick dice with girls and boys (apoká'ssini) on a schoolyard playground. She was real serious.

CHAPTER 7

The Prison Diary of Jesús Ángel Escobar

It was supposed to be some kind of vatic manifesto. A timeless ledger. For all mankind. He called it his tell-all. A spiritual timestamp honoring the desecrated, the divine, the unholy, the misshapen and mundane. An ode to the soul of *humanidad*. A configuration of *predestinación* and want. And, for that, his work would lead the way into the next millennium. His treasure would be plucked from the bowels of this very dungeon and transposed to a literary vault for future generations to read, study, and admire. They will marvel at my words, the words of el hombre, Jesús Ángel Escobar, the man.

Jesus told himself ... It will soon come to pass because it is so.

This night, he was in rarest form. He chatted away in a clouded banter. His *especial mexicano español* was fiery and fervent and full force. He prattled on. A lumpy stream of consciousness. His dialogue ... extemporaneous at best and purely undirected. There was no audience. He delivered it to no one because to him it didn't matter. There was greatness in his thought, his words, and greatness transcended all else no matter what. Pablo was proof. He was where he was and sermonized from right there high aloft his top bunk.

It was Jesus' view of Jesus ... *I am divine* ... and he was certain that he had been expressly touched by a higher power. His message, his insouciant delivery was that of a pliant preacher (drunk on his own self anointed clairvoyance) laboring from behind a lofty lectern.

Jesus, he could have been peddling rusted jalopies or hawking used kitchen utensils and clay pots from a roadside lean-to without want of another prop or need of another provision ... he found himself that convincing.

Maybe (he thought), he would call it his viewpoint on God. *Punto de Vista Sobre Dios*. Perhaps, he would label it (in a more casual approach although far less heady) his slant on religion. It could be accompanied by his dismissively flippant calculation, the grossly improbable likelihood of a supreme being, the maker of heaven and earth. He had always mocked the notion of some splendid Mexicano hereafter. After all, there was already the pontiff's *vida* not to mention *the* street merchant's *la Santa Muerte as* explanation enough. But, this was simply Jesus conjecture. There was no real surety on the *Jesus* here-and-now, much less his stretch into some great beyond, and he knew this. After all, this would come much, much later. He conceded as much since he was altogether certain that he had only begun to live out his full potential as the man, el hombre ... the convict, the bandido, el gángster, pistolero, narco, all in one and more ... La Leyenda! Like Pablo, the legend himself. Or, so he liked to think.

His prison time was coming to an end. Life would begin anew. Things could only get better. Fulfillment, real cumplimentiento, had eluded him, but it was on the way if not just around the corner.

The entire notion, these writings and entries, they were hardly thought out or premeditated (unlike his crimes) and not nearly defined enough, much less polished and poetic enough, to be labeled and drafted into a single collection as some type of treatise ... *El Tratado of Jesús Ángel Escobar*, say. But, it was, somehow most certainly, the framework of his own filosofía. He had even subtitled the work, *Realidad Manifiesto.*

It was written in longhand, drafted in pencil for easy revision even though it was as much scribble as intelligible cursive. There were broad strokes of characters and signage in and along the margins to help himself and the reader (whoever that might be) navigate their way and visualize the snippets of transient insight into the real and deeper meaning and underbelly of life itself. Death, too. Religion, as well. Not to mention his own twist on the true essence of man's inner being. It was always more Jesus on Jesus stacked end to end.

In short, it was his way of saying that he had no religión.

Pointedly, if not ultimately, Jesus believed in nothing.

Furthermore, he dared anyone to disagree. *Muerte en represalia.*

(Muerte a todus who cross me or challenge my lead. Entry #87 from earlier in this same journal entitled The Ángel's Pain, A Tribute To Cousin Pablo, Conquistador and Héroe to the Common Man.)

From his prison cell, Jesus Ángel Escobar began the short narrative this way.

Entry #271: Religión.

El Oro Del Tonto, or Fool's Gold, My Amigos.

By Jesús Ángel Escobar, prisoner at large.

I am no doubt a vassal of Christ, vasallo de Cristo, and this is The Resurrection of Jesus, my prison diary, the detailed prison diary of one Jesús Ángel Escobar, El Hombre and, by all measure, Satan's little brother (el hermanito de Satanás).

For your information, I, too, am a vasallo of El Diablo, Lucifer, the fallen cousin, el desecrated Primo of Dios Himself.

Remember this always and listen carefully to what I say. Hear me out.

Every family fights. They have their feuds and quarrels. Sometimes these things are very, very nasty and quite bitter. You know this to be true, amigos. You have seen it just as I have seen it. But, this is okay for we all, you and me as the members of the same family, we can kiss and make up later when the time comes, when the time is right ... No matter how great the transgresión. So, here it is for you to consider, my friend, and it is all true what I say so mark it down before it comes to pass.

You see the God and the devil, the fallen ángel, they are not so far apart any longer. I say that the two, this God and his cousin, the devil, El Diablo as Belcebú (Family, amigos, they are family, I swear by all the stars above.) they have kissed and made up. They are not the enemies of old, you know, the one fighting the forces of evil while the other scatters those same seeds of *maleficencia* just for fun and pleasure and to piss off the Other. Now, I say, the two, they are comrades in mischievousness. Detriment's duo.

Or, even, perhaps, the God and His Devil, they now are one and the same. Comprendes?

Okay. I know this is a great deal for you to take in. However, it is best for you to think on these things and embrace this lo antes posible.

Now. Listen some more to Jesus and what I will teach you. This is special for sure.

I see God. I really do. I see God each and every day. Of this, I am certain. Muy mucho ciertos. He is there, just as I have always suspected, just as, deep down, I have always known. Oh, sure, you say. Where do you see the God, this Dios, Jesús Ángel Escobar? You are surely blowing smoke up my butt the same way you blow the smoke from your cigarrillos and your marihuana joints. But, I say to you, no, no, no, my good friend, I do see God. I really do.

Indeed.

This God, El Dios, He sits up there on the big white cumulus cloud to the left, there ... yes, that one ... floating like a tuft of cotton over the back half of the prison yard, there beyond the razor wire and the guard tower, past the halogen flood lamps and the open field. There He is, even now. I can point Him out to you on sunny days particularly when it is hotter than hell in here, the devil's cathedral, where the flies sit lifelessly on the prisoner stench from within just waiting on one of us to die so they can finally gorge their own body weight (a hundred times over or more) in a convict's carcass.

Dios, this God-man, He sits up there and laughs His ass off at me and you and all the other miserable, madre-follondo reclusos, here in the big house. The Heavenly Chief, this El Hombre Grande, He doesn't give a rat's ass. I, personally, think that He is amused by our condición. I have seen Him with my own two eyes.

On many occasions, this God, He is like some magnífico Roman emperador at His coliseum except, with Him, it is never a thumbs up or a thumbs down. No, no, no, no. It is not like that at all ... more thumbs level (with a waggle) just to keep it going and temper the suspense of His own depravity ... you know, just for the sake of it, for His own wicked and perverse entertainment.

We, me and you, we are the *Carnaval* and the *Circo* in one. Make no mistake. I have seen the way He looks down his nose at us. This God, El Dios, He and the devil, Señor Profanado Diablo, they are really one in the same with (sadly) interchangeably grotesque and mórbida intención, one as dishonest and double-dealing as the other.

He is tripping. That is my take on it and my interpretación. Take it from me none other than Jesus Ángel Escobar himself. This is what I see and feel from my station here in life.

Tripping, you ask? Yes. That is what I say and my natural conclusión for I am stuck here just watching all the shit go down. Leroy gangin' on Leroy Number Two and Leroy Junior. Tyrell bustin' Tyrell Junior, his bitch, his pussy cellmate, for more dope or an afternoon blow job. Nazi Ned and Skinhead Fred, they are like head bangers in a heavy metal group twisting their tattoos into a knot, flexing over in between the weights and the heavy pulleys. He-men in cutoffs and do-rags and prison boots laced loose to show off their calf muscles and the rawboned script between their varicose veins and their bulbous bellies and septic scar tissue.

Then, there are the Mestizos and the proud Mayans, like me, chillin' and biding our time, tats and rats, bandanas, do rags, and rapper gear strung from beer tabs and soda cans, chillin', that is, until we break out and break free and wreak havoc on El Gringo Nation all over again ... what got us all here in the first place.

God, He just sits there and laughs at all of this. I am sure of it. I see Him clearly in the bright light of the daytime. His face is all lit up, and He is like a fat man, *un hombre gordo*, at a food *banquete*. This God, El Dios, He, too, is a cross and a hybrid, a split personality and a joker all rolled into one, my amigos. I swear it is so. This God, He is a Mister Clean, arms folded and the lone earring dangling, and sometimes, or just as often, He is a seated Buddha with the disposition of a surly komodo dragon, the whole time flicking His tongue and drooling (just like the dragon) and shifting side to side and back again ready to pounce on His unsuspecting prey (presa). And, we, me and you, my friend, we most certainly are la presa.

We should be afraid. Ciertamente again. But, too, we must stand up to this hyena, this God-hombre, El Dios, if we are to carry on. Without this, all hope is lost.

He is just fucking with you, amigo. That is all. It will not get better. Just wait and see. You are just led along, the carrot dangling in front of you, you chasing the orange stick, clippity clop, clippity clop ... el pequeño burro de Dios, you as God's little burro, my friend. You are little more to the big Man.

He has seen it all, God has. I say He touches down occasionally in the predawn like some kind of badass flying saucer from outer space, espacio exterior, grabs a dude as sacrificial lamb, then takes back off before He eats him whole with a croissant covered in orange marmalade ... then guzzles his black coffee in a wash down; it is His breakfast, my friends. The men here within, they sometimes just disappear like they never existed. Maybe on off days, He stuffs His catch in between the fold of a soft tortilla shell and covers el prisionero with chili verde and sour cream and a little pepper Jack.

Three bites, the jail bird is gone. Dios, He merely belches from the indigestion. Lifts His leg. Farts.

So, call it thunder.

Why not? I just did, and that is pretty freaking funny you have to admit.

That is God, my amigo. It is who He is. Like the marriage ... it is for better or worse.

And, I am Jesús Ángel Escobar, el hombre, the vasallo de Cristo, and el hermanito de Satanás, writing in my little diary about the hell that I live in twenty-four seven for it is what I know.

But, soon, very, very soon, I am to be released. My time here is almost up. I will be finished living in between the crosshairs of the devil, amigos. Mañana, I will go free.

And then? (I hear you ask.)

I am back. Doing the do. Loping the mule. Flogging the dog. Beating el gato. Slapping the mistress (before she gets out of line), not to mention the wife. Strumming my vihuela and singing my sad, depressing (dipremente canción) song, as well. And, no less, back to fucking with the world at large, the same world that has been fucking with me for all these many years. Finally, I can leave my imprint on the planet once and for all like a bear paw on soft earth. Resucitado for sure.

Some people think that I am loco. Está loco. Yes, they call me that ... but never to my face.

Who me? I ask always as playfully.

Quien, yo? Le pido ... is what I say in my lovely, native tongue.

Me, Jesús Escobar? Loco? (Repartee, my friend, repartee. My sweet innocence knows no bounds.)

Hah! I say. No way. No es posible. It is me, Jesús Ángel Escobar, your mejor amigo of all time. I would not harm you. I come in the name of Jesús Cristo, remember? For we are both the sons of God. Like twins joined at the hip.

Jesus laughed the loudest of his jail day; he was giddy in his discovery, joyous at the grandiloquent expression of his own free will as he read aloud his findings back to himself. He yipped and whooped insanely. Next, he trilled like a mating cicada, all of this in time with the trailing echo from the other side of the corridor wall.

"Resurrected," he said aloud. *"Resucitado."*

A voice yelled back from out of the dark, "Shut the fuck up and go to sleep, you crazy Mexican."

So, Jesus retreated. He quietly retired to his journal drafting figures in the adjacent margin, filling the empty spaces top and bottom, left and right. Soon, he would be set free. In his vision, a softer vision, he would hitchhike to another town, kill a man, steal his belongings, and begin life anew.

CHAPTER 8

Ksistsikam Ayikinaan
A Voice from Nowhere

(Blackfeet Translation)

From his position behind long binoculars, a man stood relaxed and watched. He was adjacent and cozied up to a black, late model sedan. The car was parked in a supple but unapparent bend in a country crossroad. There was enough of a fixed undulation in the mix so that it left one road hidden from the other adjoining it. The layout made the man's position more of a perch. It was loftier than the surface around him yet hidden from view by anyone else, unsuspecting or otherwise, and from all directions. The man hadn't planned this as a stop-off. Hardly. Nothing about it was devised. It was purely impromptu. Yet, had he, the spot where he found himself, couldn't have been more perfect. Corn stalks more than trees. Enough brush as cover and as a whole. The stubble trees bare yet stacked in a back to back sequence did the trick as camouflage. He was even down wind, not that his scent or scent of any kind really mattered.

The two had designated themselves Caller 1 & Caller 2 as though they were secret agents from the wrong side of illicit and nonconformity. Crypto-kings, spy gods, a couple of coded and secretive brigands, nefarious to the core and on the sly abridging their own wry mix of avant-garde art theft and stolen property, it was the way they saw themselves. The surreptitious details of their plot and their connivance had convinced them of their own high-minded intent. This in turn, they believed, could or would lead to some extraordinary level of high end $ucce$$. Yes, of course, the garish symbol spelling was for all the world to see ... the spelling as logo, the logo as vanity tag. For security purposes, the two disposed of cell phones as frequently as tableware from an all-night diner countertop leaving no trace of a trail much less their furtive intentions or whereabouts. At present, they were simply dug in and waiting.

Out on Jackson Highway again. Seven miles North, beyond where Jesus Escobar stood, the two men identified themselves as caller ID #1 (This was a man named City Chief) who talked to the man identified as caller ID #2. Caller #2, he was left unnamed. Caller #1, City Chief, he spoke low in a clipped cadence with his back's reflection ... wet, combed hair, dark jacket, narrow physique ... outlined on the dark tinted windshield of the car that he was driving.

"Any sign of D'Artagnan?" said City Chief.

"No. Nothing," said Caller #2 to City Chief.

"What is he driving?" asked City Chief.

"A sedan," said Caller #2. "Black. Or, dark navy. Gold rims. Mercedes. Early to late model. Used I'm sure."

"Okay," said caller City Chief. "We'll wait." He continued, "You're sure we're on the right road."

"Yes," says Caller #2. "Ninety nine percent sure. Two turns between here and where he was last spotted. Both dead end dirt roads. Ninety nine percent sure. No guarantees in life. You know that, boss. Death and taxes, death and taxes, boss."

"Taxes are for the faint of heart. Can't speak to death. I'll meet you further on up the road," said the man, City Chief.

The man looked away, looked back into his own cell phone #1 again, and then looked broadly into the distance once more searching for clues.

"Is that D'Artagnan?" asked the first caller.

"Yes," said the second. "I'm pretty sure that's D'Artagnan."

"Who is in the car with D'Artagnan?" asked the man. This lone observer named City Chief pointed into the distant road out and over the curve of his binocular lens with his index finger like he was following a fast-moving predator, say a graceful and fixated feline, a big cat, a leopard, a lioness, a cheetah, behind the camera's wide aperture. The man, he was tall and as sleek as his finger was smooth and deliberate in its movement.

From cell #2. The other man answered: "I don't know. Don't recognize him."

The man is a long way off but near enough so the two see the same thing.

From cell phone #1. "He is a Mexican?" The man is almost surprised but simply wants to clarify the observation (ditto) from such a distance.

The response again from cell phone #2 came in clear: "Appears so." He, too, looked through long binoculars from atop a different plateau, a berm the size of a misappropriated pillbox. A different black sedan, slightly smaller but similar in shape, sleeker. The caller on cell phone #2 was not nearly as relaxed. He was sweaty palmed, apprehensive even fidgety. He saw what he saw for different reasons but wanted to see the same thing that cell phone #1 saw.

From cell phone #1. "Who is he? Better yet, where did he come from?"

From cell phone #2: "Again," he looking deeper into the lenses like an answer will simply appear, but it doesn't. "Don't know," he replies.

From cell phone #1, the man says, "He isn't supposed to be here." There was a pause from cell phone #1. A sweep of wind gust into the cell mic, then, "Kill him," breaks the silence between the two.

The answer back from cell phone#2 is, "Okay."

The man with cell phone #2 squared himself over the roof of the black sedan, raised the rifle from the scabbard to a careful stature, and positioned it across his shoulder, to his chin, his eye flexed to a squint to the sight, he curled his finger into the trigger's curve, breathed coolly twice, then fired. He looked out front. D'Artagnan's car has stopped in a roll, but not from the gunshot. Something else was amiss. The sideview mirror splattered in the evening air. The gun shot from back there, where cell phone #1 and cell phone #2 were, was hardly noticeable. The glass and chrome were scattered everywhere on the ground. The Mexican looked around hurriedly, they can see him and all this from the distance, then he slams the trunk lid, and hurriedly moves back inside the car behind the wheel. It's not where he was. He wasn't the driver. Pretty sure, thinks cell phone #1. *Ditto* that, thinks cell phone #2.

"What the hell?" said the caller. The caller City Chief said it again the same way. "What the hell?" This time with greater disbelief.

The man from cell phone #2 simply replied: "Don't know. Nothing. No one's moving."

From cell phone #1, the man City Chief said, "The Mexican, he's now running around the back. Dragging something. Try again."

There was no response from cell phone #2, just another shot. It rang out across the hollow.

"The Mexican's back in the car again. He's driving off. Shoot him," said caller #1.   "Shoot the son of a bitch. D'Artagnan, too, wherever he is? Do you see D'Artagnan? (No answer in the still.) Shoot them both and shoot them now."

CHAPTER 9

The Painting in The Trunk of the Car

Jesus finally took notice of the dead man's call. The cell phone (D'Artagnan's) was sitting on the passenger car seat open faced where the dead man had left it. In the meantime, Jesus Escobar drove with both hands, eyes front and fixed. He hadn't noticed much less thought about the cell until it started ringing over and over and over ... *Frère Jacques, Frère Jacques, dormez-vous? Dormez-vous? Frère Jacques, Frère Jacques, dormez-vous? Dormez-vous?*... though it was as much warble as melody. Besides, Jesus Escobar, the newly released prisoner, had been preoccupied, smiling, perspiring, lost in thought, and reliving the events of the moments just before when he had been too busy loading a dead man into the trunk of his car, ducking gunshots from out of nowhere, and driving away from the scene of his own crime not to mention the unstated crimes of the other unknowns surrounding him.

Hola, outside world! He had only just spoken to himself. *And, hola again to you Jesús Ángel Escobar, my old friend. Welcome back,* he said. *For sure, I am now alive again and back to the life that was once my own. This adrenilina circling in my veins, it is magnifico and pure magic within my soul.*

Even as he spoke this and smiled again to himself, he drove very hurriedly down an unfamiliar highway because he was still in every possible way uncertain, nervous, and tense … feverishly alive, yes, for certain, but frazzled and jittery, and somehow disjointedly lucid and focused. The mix of chaos, mayhem, and trickery, it leveled him out, like goodness to a saint. After all, it was Jesús Ángel Escobar, and he was now once again completed and the Jesus of old.

When Jesus answered the call, the voice of a man said, "D'Artagnan? D'Artagnan, is that you?"

Jesus said, "No. This is not D'Artagnan. D'Artagnan, he is in the back."

"Well, let me speak to D'artagnan," said the voice of the man on the other end.

"D'Artagnan can't come to the phone right now," said Jesus.

"Well, who in the hell is this?" said the same voice.

"This is Jesus," said Jesus. "Jesús."

"Who?" said the man.

"Jesus," said Jesus again. "Jesús Ángel Escobar."

"And, who the hell are you, Jesus Ángel Escobar?" said the man on the other end. "I am a friend of D'Artagnan," said Jesus. "Me and D'Artagnan, we are old friends. We go way back. We are business partners, too. One in the same."

"Let's cut to the chase, Jesus Ángel Escobar," said the voice on the other end. "Does D'Artagnan still have my painting?"

The painting: *The Resurrection of Jesus* was engraved on the backside. When the picture was turned over, it looked like this.

In the lower left-hand corner of the painting, the crown of thorns had been cast aside. It was a setting nestled amongst a bed of faint yellow-golden lilies at the bank of a dark, still-blue pool of water. Something like a pond yet smaller.

"I see you've been moving things around in D'Artagnan's car," said the caller, "so you must know what's going on.

"Si," said Jesus. "Si, we still have the painting. That is right. The painting, la pintura, it is here. Que es correcto. It is safe and sound and along for the ride."

In the upper right-hand corner, opposite the crown of thorns, was a halo of broken sunlight shining through a deliberate bank of dark clouds. It was the intended contrast of dark to light and light back to dark as artist preference and intention. It was more subtle than in other previous works, but it was there. Jesus, the Risen Jesus, was cast in a dim veil of tawdry earth tones, his pale skin fragmented and cast against beaded rays of an intermittent and frail refraction, but it was clear and unmistakable that it was the Christ child as the man, crucified, dead, buried and now risen. With one open palm and two feet scarred from driven spikes, there was no doubt.

"However," said Jesus Escobar, "this painting since it is in our possession at this moment in time, maybe it is no longer your painting, amigo. Comprendes?"

Jesus smiled.

"Listen, you son of bitch," said the voice, "Let's get this straight. The painting you and D'Artagnan are packing around belongs to me. I'm not sure where you are, but you need to stop what you're doing and deliver the painting back to its rightful owner before things get really heated. Do you understand, Jesus whoever you are?"

"Yes," said Jesus. "Entiendo. I understand. Sí. However, D'Artagnan and I, D'Artagnan y yo, we have discussed this for many hours, mucho, mucho horas, mi amigo, and we believe that it is only right that we share in the reward of such a valuable piece of artwork that we have helped to preserve. Wouldn't you agree?"

"Listen, you filthy little rodent," said the man.

Jesus hung up.

CHAPTER 10

Coming Full Circle

The Vatican Loaner in a Three-part Switcheroo

Forty-five minutes had passed.

Jesus drove.

The Quick Locker was two doors down from Johnny's Supper Club and across the street from Elba's Beauty Salon. It was a bad part of town but close enough to the YMCA where Jesus had just booked a room with a fifteen-dollar deposit (D'Artagnan's fifteen dollars) and a fake ID (D'Artagnan's as well). Jesus parked the car, D'Artagnan's stolen sedan, on the shade side of the street two spaces down from a yellow fire hydrant. He lifted the picture _ frame, blanket wrap, and all _ from the back seat, tucked it under his arm, and walked into The Quick Locker. He paid the man behind the caged window ten dollars (from D'Artagnan's wallet), a month's rent, and pushed the key into his trouser pocket and walked to aisle K. He stood in front of locker 59. He slid the painting _ frame, picture, blanket, and the works _ into locker 59 Row K closed the door, tested the door for secure, and walked out.

I am a free man, he thought. He figured his leg up on the future was in locker 59. As it stood, things had only come full circle in three circuitous moves.

The Vatican Loaner Switcheroo Part 1.

Hours before, a young woman had walked into The Quick Locker. She appeared quite disheveled in both appearance and apparel. She carried both a gravely overwrought demeanor and a croker sack that read *Buckeye Cottonseed Meal* in a faded, tall-stenciled lettering. In it was a blanket-wrapped, framed picture, unvalued but priceless. Cradling the frame with her one arm left the backside of the painting partially exposed, exposed enough for the inscription to be seen or read as *The Resurrection of Jesus. E*ven in the poorly lit storefront entry, you could almost make out the signature although, as circumstance would dictate, it wouldn't be seen by anyone nearby or in the offing. Tucking the fold of the blanket back into place to conceal her questionable chattel and its title, the woman went to the caged window and asked to rent a locker. She was given locker # 59.

"Row J," said the attendant. "Row J."

Twice he called this out, *Row J*, like some short-order cook in a busy, smelly and cheap, late night eatery even though there was no one else there.

"Not Row I," he added as she continued to move away. "And, not Row K," he said on top of that. "Row J," he said again.

It was like he was stacking pancakes.

For ten dollars, she, too, got a month's worth of space and a small key the width and length of a midwife's thimble. She walked to Row J near the big picture window and stood in front of locker # 59. She opened it with the key. She placed the blanket-wrapped, framed picture into locker # 59, closed the door, tested the door for secure, turned, stuffed her dress deeper into the waist of her jeans, redressed her boot straps in a bend, straightened up, tossed her hair back, and walked out the front door. Outside, she looked down once into the palm of her hand to make sure she had the key. She did. She, then, tucked it into her trouser pocket for safekeeping.

In another moment, she was whisked away in a black sedan without incident.

The Vatican Loaner Switcheroo Part 2.

Shortly thereafter, a man, he was of average height and build, a musk-colored Negro wearing matching black French beret, turtleneck, trousers, and shiny, new, lace-up Florsheim shoes, walked into The Quick Locker. He appeared on the one hand quite wary, however, seemed just as evenly intent on showing a settled and cavalier moxie and an almost devil-may-care insouciance simply by virtue of the fact that he had shown up.

Before walking into the shop, he had been parked across the street for some time and watched through the large plate glass window at the front of the building as the young woman with the croker sack stored her belongings in locker # 59 Row J. When the door swiveled to fully open, the number was quite visible, even in plain view, through his binoculars rolled to a polished and pristine focus and peeking over the obtuse crack in the driver-side window. It was the reason he knew to ask for rental Locker # 59. He heard himself say casually, convincingly to the attendant,

"Locker 59 Row J, if you don't mind. it's my lucky number and always has been. J's my mother's maiden name."

The cashier plainly was not interested. He said that Locker # 59 had been rented already and went back to reading his horoscope. The man had folded it at the corner's edge of his daily newspaper.

Then, the black man, the Negro in the black French beret, said,

"Well, then, locker number 60 will have to do I suppose."

He paid the cashier in small bills and pocket change, further angled his beret (askance if not histrionically) above his breached eyebrow and walked to the third aisle and stood in front of Locker # 59 and Locker # 60. He took a hair pin from the corner of his beret and quickly worked it, curvature side up, into the keyhole. He pried open the keyed lock on Locker # 59, placed the contents into a used Army blanket, shifted the locks from 59 to 60 and 60 to 59, secured the two, turned, and walked out without even so much as a passing glance to the cashier behind the plate glass. He had what he came for and, most importantly, what he felt he was owed.

Outside, he walked the thirty paces that he closely counted (self awareness or paranoia, interpreter's view) and placed the army blanket and contents into the trunk of his dark sedan, a nearly late model Mercedes. With fixed intent, he made a u turn and drove off into the afternoon cold.

On the drive, the man, the black man now lifting the French beret from his scalp and capturing his reflection in the rearview mirror, said aloud and proudly to himself, "My mother said to me that I was born blacker than a moonless night, yet more fanciable than the solstice sun."

D'Artagnan du Vitet, the St. Bart's-to-Boston bon vivant, the curator's custodian, and single-handed yegg, was at once lost in the moment in his most mesmerizing and prideful thought because success was as suddenly his.

CHAPTER 11

D'Artagnan du Vitet

Of Pride, Prejudice, & Happenstance.
The life and times of the curator's custodian cut short.

I am D'Artagnan, and I was D'Artagnan when we met. He was introduced to me as City Chief, and as I recall, he introduced himself. That's all that I knew then, and it is all that I know now.

We met because we met, and that was it. There was no other reason.

We didn't meet because some acquaintance or other mutual friend introduced us. We certainly didn't meet because a higher power came to each of our rescue. Nor, did we meet because, say, we bumped into one another due to some offload from a neutral and obscure corner quadrangle in a downtown office enclosure voided us, like two hackers in cinque, and simultaneously spit us into that particular space and time of a late afternoon's traffic and big city, pedestrian mayhem. No. We met because we met. It was coincidental. I accepted that fact, and if I have accepted that fact, then so can you. For better or worse let's just say and then move on.

I never saw it as a setup as some have suggested. In my view, there was no grander purpose. There was no great intent or greater intent or greatest intent either. It simply came together and came to pass. In a trickle, in a charge, through fastidious melancholy, maybe out of furious boredom ... it's so difficult to say. I'm not one to grant more meaning to things than they deserve particularly those things that just happen. A sunny day, a rainy day, windy, balmy, stormy, blustery, or calm, this entire episodic mess simply took shape like the moment's sunset or a passing mood. But, things simply broke this way and not that, and with that, I'm satisfied. Possibly, it was just as well looking back. And so, *it* happened. *It* just was. (Or, wasn't, said a friend.) Call *it* what you want.

There was no *raison d'être* as reason for being.

Rationalize in rations, that's what I do.

As a great sage once said: *things happen.* So be it, say I, and move on.

To the Biblically-minded (my mother was sometimes one), erstwhile happenstance is too feeble and fraught with misdeed and lack of purpose to satisfy their unquenchable need for answers. (Always, there must be answers. I can hear her say, *Quick! An explanation, for god's sake! Courtiers, bring me answers!* Like she was lordly or Elizabethan even, her ... the pretentiously well-heeled commoner from the tiny little Quanalao island no less.) The believers can't handle the plainness and gravity-less dictum of pure chance. To them, it's unappealing; some would say appalling. It's not tidy. It's not clean. It's not simple enough or gut wrenching enough in the offing. It has to be made endearing and cute. Shouldn't it somehow, some way, say, be tied up in a bright and pretty bow?

No, not by a long shot, say I, D'Artagnan du Vitet. For it is that same implausible wager that cracks or carries all of human existence.

When things break and go our way, it *is* God's plan. All praise be to the Big Fellow, the Grand Illusionist, the Master Magician, the Potentate and Purveyor of smoke-cured, honey glazed happy endings.

When things go the other direction, against us, what then?

Why, you are little more than a pint-sized Job, well-heeled in the cacophony and truculence of half-baked misgivings, resolute mistrust, not to mention your own incriminating miscalculation. You, too, are then little more than a tar-feathered, luckless dolt, or worse still, one sorry-fied derelict left mortified and homeless in a single throw of life's loaded dice.

But, what the hey? It's all that any of us have left for the time being while in the middle of the grand and imposing fracas ... its sweep and grind.

D'Artagnan thought aloud as he pointed to the sky, "I dare *You*, Captain Almighty. I double dare *You*. Fuck me on this one, and I'm done with *You* forever ... in spite of my mother's own most devout shake and bake rosary reclamations. *Ball's in your court, Father Fate.*"

CHAPTER 12

The Tables Turned

Looking back again at his perfectly cast reflection, D'Artagnan patted both his cheeks and smiled a smile for all the world to see. Know this, he thought soothingly to himself, this is my most prideful moment.

He, as soon, settled back and remembered fondly the loving touch of his mother (a plaçage creole as was her legend), her tender voice, and listening once again to her adoration and admiration for her round-faced, black baby boy, for he was most certainly her most perfect creation of all time.

"In those first weeks, she said that I looked most beautiful propped up against a backdrop of white linen and island pastels in her rope hammock on the open porch. She said that I was spectacular. *Spectacular*. Her word. I was her *chocolate morsel*, her *cocoa drop and daytime's dimple of delight*.

The linen … it highlighted not only my complexion but my round features as well.

That is what she said. Why, I can hear her somber and soothing voice speaking to me now.

Particularly, there was such conviction in her Barthélemy brogue that it makes my spine tingle and bristle with pride to this very day

... particularly, she said, my big, brown eyes. When they opened, she said they were wider, more revealing and grander than the Gustavian dawn itself. She swore that she could see God's soul right there in the cradle of her arms. I remember it so well. That is what she said and said it all with such verve that I can still feel the emotion as though it had movement, the love a curvature, the generosity a color and a shape of its own. When she held me close to her, she said that my smile was a beacon second only to sunlight itself.

"Mama du Vitet," said D'Artagnan into the highway drone, "you would be so proud of me now. Look at what I have gone and done."

D'Artagnan smiled grandly; he had finished his highway soliloquy.

D'Artagnan du Vitet purposefully, steadily, and calmly pulled his sedan to the side of the road past its shoulder. Here, he could better concentrate and carry out his plan. He picked up his cell phone and dialed out. With one hand on the steering wheel, the other on the receiver, his view fixed on the open horizon, and the engine humming in idle, he spoke aloud. It was nothing short of stunted exuberance and restrained transcendence. He thought ... *I have pulled it off,* and then repeated to himself excitedly ... *I have. I have truly pulled it off.* He could feel his own special glow as he grinned.

When the other caller answered, D'Artagnan began.

"So, here I am, Chief," he said nervously.

He was giddy as well.

He then measurably paused.

"It is me. D'Artagnan. (As if you didn't know.) I am smiling to myself and driving my car lickety split down this open blacktop in a breakneck getaway that was certainly meant to be. It is destiny, City, truly destiny. And, destiny at its finest. Wouldn't you agree, City Chief, my boy? At least by my calculation. And, my calculation is all that matters to me at this moment in time. So, it is, and, so be it, too."

He paused only to draw a breath and begin again knowing full well that the man on the other end of the call was still intently listening to his every word, his every inflection, the naked and bifurcated sarcasm, as well as the bend and lilt of his sardonic twists and taunts.

"I have worked tirelessly all my life, Chief, my dear man. And, sad to say, I have nothing whatsoever to show for it.

But, really now. What *is* a custodian to a curator to do? And, what is a custodian to a curator anyway? I mean in the grand scheme of things, City my boy? And, as you well know and I well know and the whole wide world well knows, it is nothing more than a rhetorical question, because we both know the answer is: *Nothing.*

We all know that nothing begets nothing. We know, as well, that nothing times nothing is nothing, and added to nothing is still nothing ... nada, zilch, null set, and in all actuality is less than zero itself. I would describe it more or less like a pin prick on the open abyss of one's own curiously undefined black hole.

Wouldn't you agree, Mister Chief, sir?"

D'Artagnan never intended to let the listener answer or to get so much as a cleft response. He had the upper hand so he continued.

"Let me expound," he said.

"Call the temp agency, and you can easily get another *knee-grow.*

Make another call and you can just as easily get another *home-boy* or a dish rag or two or three, maybe even a Mongol to displace the others on the cheap, someone say just to mop the floors and scour your pots not to mention the pans. Or, say, set up a museum for the take while you take all the proceeds, the credit, and the cash or in short you collect all the dough. Sound familiar?

Double, double, toil and trouble, and all that jazz.

But, you know that, too, City Chief. And, you knew that when you cut me out of the spoils of our heist ... even though it was the heist that I, and I alone, set up for you. And, perfectly, I might add.

I was the expendable knee-grow. In time, you no doubt thought I would go away and fall through the cracks. But, alas, you were wrong, and here we are. But most importantly, here I am."

"You stiffed me, Chiefy Chief," said D'Artagnan on the exhale. "And, shame on you."

There was still no reply or engagement on the other end, but D'Artagnan knew his listener was there. Money was at stake and lots of it. And, money *does* talk. It listens, too. This was living proof.

D'Artagnan took a deeper breath to sink his verbal dagger deeper and continued in well metered syncopation.

"I have watched you two ... you and that bonny, little female hyena of yours; tits and ass not to mention the sass ... from a distance, but I can and will watch no more. I bartered for your trust. And, sadly, I delivered in spades. (Pun intended, white boy.)"

D'Artagnan felt justly pushed to bigotry ... the same bigotry that was his inalienable right and subliminal recourse. He'd learned it early on. He thanked his mother every day.

'Tis your God given right, but the white boy's blight. Make it so,' she'd say. He, D'Artagnan, recounted her pitiless venom. *'Bigotry is ours, a weapon for plundering, it's bounty so plentiful in the offing it leaves the white man defenseless and subjugated by virtue of his own guilt. Never let up, dear boy. Never.'*

Dire straits, inclement weather, trial and tribulation, abject bill collection ... all moments that he, D'Artagnan, could and should feel pushed to bigotry to forego his own responsibility. Hardly his fault, certainly no shame. Use it or lose it. Per se, fate's indebtedness to the disenfranchised-set-free. He was never at fault. No black man (each and every one an old-time Negro) could be blamed much less held culpable or accountable for hate's revenge and kindness' remorse. It was, again, his indisputable, incontestable truth as calling card ... a wild card no less ... #53, played at a whim in time of need or just in time to gain the upper hand.

He drew another and stronger breath.

"In return for my fairmindedness, I was flagrantly double-crossed like never before in my miserable, meaningless little life.

How dare you, City Chief? You and your little side tramp of an infectious vamp.

(A little Island rap for you, art con-boy.)

You gained access to my gallery.

(Why, I had just dusted and waxed the front entry floor that very morning.)

You cherry-picked the cream of the crop that I selected for you, and you, then, pilfered the goods that I handpicked and laid out for you like presents on Christmas morn, and, worse yet, you greedily demanded a higher cut from our original handshake.

To top it all off, you made off into the night free and clear and unscathed and untraceable again, all at my election.

And then, of all things … of all the most improbable and impossible things that one could ever imagine … you betrayed me and tossed me aside like I was last year's decoration, the week before's leftovers, or paper wrappings from an unwanted gift at someone else's farewell party.

I must admit I was fooled.

Worse than that, I was made the fool.

But, never fear and careful what you wish for, Sir Chieftain, I am the fool no more.

D'Artagnan is riled, resurrected, and revitalized, and riding down this lonely, rickety highway with *our* Vatican prize in the trunk of *my* car.

Without me, you two hoodlums are a pair of petty crooks, two, want-a-be art thieves, stumble-bums at best, groping about hopelessly, helplessly in the wee hours and the dead of night tripping over shrubbery, English ivy, sprinkler heads, iron grates, drain covers, welcome-less welcome mats, and yourselves all the while pretending to be the big time cracksmen you aren't, weren't, and never will be.

I am more jilted than a basket full of some philanderer's unsuspecting old loves, mistresses, and concubines. Faking fidelity never works, City. You should know that by now.

Make no mistake, the two of you, you and your misty Shawnee Mae, you owe me this treasure of a jewel in my possession from the last heist and in the worst way.

The art in the trunk of my car will certainly more than even the score since I did not receive my fair share. As I recall, it was a share that you had so handsomely and eloquently promised.

'One third, D'Artagnan, oh, most assuredly, one third,' is what *you* said.

'Couldn't begin to *do it without you, you and your astute cunning and guile, D'Artagnan, my good man*,' you said in meeting number two.

'Our master strategist,' you added. I believe it was either meeting four or five, but who's counting at this juncture.

So, one third is what we had agreed upon and finalized the day before the break-in if memory serves me correctly. But, what does it matter and who cares. Let bygones be bygones I say.

'What's fair is fair.' I believe those were your words, unkind sir.

This piece (in the trunk) will cover your debit, Sir City. It will, as well, cover the interest owed, the malice aforethought dredged up and inflicted, my pain and suffering (Woe is me ... the sleepless nights of plotting my revenge, City Chief), not to mention the attorney fees (were this a legitimate and bona fide transaction) that would have cost me a fortune, and the octuple overtime accumulated in planning overruns for me to get back to breakeven up to this point.

Presently, all is rectified, Mister City Chief.

God's in his heaven, all's right with the world."

D'Artagnan smiled looking out over the windshield. As he pulled back onto the highway, he felt triumphant, vindicated, and heroic. From inside his car, he listened and waited for an answer, but there was no answer. He waited, drew another stronger breath, and then spoke clearly into his cell for the last time.

"Chief, I have the painting. Or, should I say, I have *my* painting that was supposed to be *our* painting. Friends for life, you said.

A friend in need is friendless indeed ... Go ahead, you can quote me.

This is payback for the money you owed me from the last job." He listened, but not really, and as soon continued. "Once again, I have the painting. I repeat, C'est *la vengeance*. This is *payback*. Nothing less. Hopefully a great deal more. So long and au revoir, City boy. All's well, that ends well, monsieur.

Oh, one last thing.

In the words of that old Negro spiritual, I, D'Artagnan du Vitet, am now, finally, and forever more ... *Free at last. Free at last. Thank God almighty I am free at last.*"

As quickly, D'Artagnan's voice had vanished.

"D'Artagnan!" said City Chief demandingly. As quickly, he then began to raise his voice and shout. "D'Artagnan, do you hear me? You'll pay for this, D'Artagnan, so help me God!"

D'Artagnan was away.

In twenty minutes behind the wheel of his car, inside the resurgence and renewal of his own destiny, D'Artagnan du Vitet inexplicably (it was an impromptu gesture to say the least) pulled over to the shoulder of the road to offer a hitchhiker a ride. In the doing (he thought), he surprised even himself. He never stopped to pick up hitchhikers, and yet his sedan almost skidded to a halt.

"No, in the back," he said motioning to the man standing roadside out in the cold. Perhaps, he himself had felt only a short time ago the way the hitchhiking transient looked ... cold, desperate, and alone ... and that lent to this offhanded, split second, if not questionable decision. Nevertheless, D'Artagnon unlocked the rear car door and waited for a moment until the stranger had climbed in and convincingly closed the rear door of the dark sedan behind him only to call out flippantly, "All aboard," in a most splendid and upbeat fashion. However, it would be D'Artagnan's last sportive gesture. He locked his vision onto the highway up ahead, and the two drove off.

CHAPTER 13

Jesus Sketches

Somewhat Obliquely ...
His victims he sketched in an embellished charcoal.

His work was too veiled for morbid. It was, as well, too detailed for macabre. A startling accuracy no matter the subject. Lifelike in death. Always at the scene. There was a stack of a dozen or so beneath a battered sketch board. The clip that held the paper to the board was mangled. However, with a twist and a bend and a bit of reshaping, it still worked.

The first ... She was a dead woman. Call her princess or princess narco. Whichever. She was an incredible likeness of herself in death on Jesus Escobar's canvas. Her dark eyes opened wide, her lips frozen, her tongue displaced, misplaced moreover, toward the corner of her mouth like she had un-finished the lick of her lip from the taste of a sweet and succulent strawberry, caught in a photo still, or perhaps her tongue had missed the trace of garnishment from a slender serving spoon ... thick, white cream dense enough to chew, certainly slurp. Her bullet wound was unapparent. (In the front, out the back.) Nearly bloodless. He'd captured that, too. A fragment of torn cloth ... that was all. Her legs had folded themselves quite neatly in the fall, a coordinated collapse like a card table or a small tent, just after her life spilled out into thin air the way that it does in the time of death. She was quite shapely ... inclined even toward the voluptuous. Her youth was figured in along her grounded outline, her corpse. She was ordered to be killed. There was no one present at the time. Executed when and where she'd been recognized by the likeness to her photograph.

After she died (a single gunshot, but a magnum shell), Jesus had gathered his belongings and placed them (pistol, silencer, bullet box, empty shells) into a carryall. He went to the outside through the open door, rummaged about in the back seat of his car, and found the case of paints, charcoal sticks beside an open sketchbook, and three brushes strapped to an art board. He walked back inside and pulled up a straight back chair and began to assemble everything, the ingredients for best results. In such a short, hurried sitting (you would think), he surely must have dutifully stuck out his thumb (yes, as if to pull out a plum) and glanced over it, once, twice, thrice, a fourth time or two, in a full, one-eyed, good measure before putting pencil to paper. Of course, it wasn't like she was going anywhere. Understood. But, from that angle, he drew her. She was an uncanny still likeness of herself for certain.

The second someone ... he was a man, a Mexicano in complimentary business attire. He was quite pale. Very, very pale to be exact and flushed of all color. The blood had left his face in a deluge his wound had been so traumatic and large, it was as though he had been impaled by a blunt fireman's pole through brute force or as though his feet had been swiftly severed machete-style and as quickly washed away while the rest of him was left dangling from a steep, seaside overhang. Blood was everywhere and all around. By the time Jesus pulled up his chair (he'd tiptoed over the dark, reddish-purple spots in the soft carpet), the murder victim looked ghostly as well as unkempt. The surprise (no, not shock; it happened too quickly) was still on his face ... ambushed from behind in close quarters ... he'd had no time to draw his own gun to defend himself

... to improvise or retort ... no time to protest ... grunt or gasp. This man, he had lived his life as a careful and cautious man, a clandestine and closet criminal (desperado), a bureaucrat by trade so it was hard to imagine there was so much blood in the element of surprise. But, so it goes. Boom. He was dead. Boom, boom, boom, boom ... he was dead ... drained and bloodless with blood all round.

After all, they were all dead. But Jesus, he would sit there pencil in hand, the oversized pad in his lap, and just draw like nothing had happened ... like he was uninvolved ... absolved, a professional observer setting the stage with its requisite dummy props and stage wares. A line, a brush stroke here, a velvety backstroke there, a forehead, a hairline, a brow, the template of two matching eyes, and sure enough ... voila! His victim captured in still life ... (oh, what a nasty if not distasteful pun) ... for all posterity by the man who'd laid them to their final rest. Later, from memory in the late hours, he transferred the image to canvas. No, not a transmogrification (transfiguración). Not at all. He hated the term. This was gentler, certainly less grotesque, well meaning if to murder someone could ever be described as *well meaning*. Perversity has its own vernacular. He preferred pastels over chalk, violet to rose, cerulean juxtaposed against earth tones and lavender. It made their faces return to life. He said so in his makeshift studio, the ten by twelve heap of throwaway magazines and newspapers amid piles of saturated painter rags crusty from brush wipes long since dried and setup as hard as mortar on a portable, rusted-out cement mixer.

The third man, he was a corpulent soul ... Jesus considered him a portrait of sorts and had propped up the dead man in the chair quite graciously after dragging him around the corner from outside the doorway. He was heavy. Dead weight. A clumsy carry. Smelly. Foul actually. He was unbathed death with grimy cuticles and dirt in the folds of his flesh, elbows and armpits, even between the creases of his unshaven neck. Pressing the air from his lungs was as rank as stagnant water at the edge of a serpent's den. When the dead man sat straight up in a lean with his back against the vinyl, his earlobes appeared larger than a baby's feet.

Jesús Escobar pushed and plied and mushed his cheeks together to form an awkward yet complacent smile. He combed the dead man's hair straight back away from his open eyes and made a simulated part from the mat of black strands. The man's eyes remained open, a small blessing. However, that wasn't the problem ... his eyes were. They were gray and colorless. It made him hard to figure ... at least from the artist's point of view ... because a man, a woman, their character was predicated on the color and sparkle of the eyes. Jesus, el artista, liked to imagine his subjects, the dead, as famous people, important, witty and clever, wealthy or wealthier than rich, and wholly independent of death itself. Their story would live on after he drew the outline of the motionless and complaisant corpse and later disposed of the body as if they, even to this day, lingered among us in some town square or city plaza while that same voice might still be heard from an empty alleyway or an open window nearby.

The third man he went into a ditch in an open field. The Sinaloa buzzards had begun to circle like flies before Jesús Ángel Escobar drove away. The man in the field, the dead man, he was heavy. Remember, too ... smelly. When Jesus gripped the steering wheel, the odor of the dead man still lay on his hands.

In his most private soliloquy, he repeatedly quoted himself ... *I am el gran maestre ... el Rembrandt Mexicano ... and a prisoner only in my time and of my consequence and circumstance.* Circunstancia be damned.

"In point of fact, it might be said that this Jesús Ángel Escobar, hombre and fugitivo, was quite the painter, el pintor and artista," said the Federale who had arrived with his diputados a week and four days too late to capture their suspect. But, he had uncovered the artist's personal colección stacked orderly and in single file even as it had been abandoned in a shady corner just inside the ramshackle

porch. *"Magnifico,"* said the man. *"This in spite of the subject matter,"* he added placing another dead man's portrait to one side.

He no sooner finished his comment than he as quickly winced and turned his head away.

By this time, Jesús Ángel Escobar had long since left the territorio and had slipped across the border north by way of the big river under dark clouds and the imperceptible night.

CHAPTER 14

Jesus Saves!

*F*rom what I can recall, this is pretty much what Jesus told me later. We were in the motel. It was the first time I heard this part of the story. It's probably not word for word, but it's real close. So, here goes.

Knew this guy that knew this guy. The second guy, he was a good guy to know. (Jesus talking here.)

Jesus said, "Go to Montana."

Handed the fellow standing there in front of him a wad of cash tied up with a thick rubber band. Then, told him to put it in the side pocket of the duffel. Duffel's in the front seat of the car. Plenty of money for gas. Money for you both is what Jesus said. Said get off at Great Falls. Take Route 89 across the face of the Rockies until you come out the other side of Glacier. You're in Babb. Go to the Babb Bar. This is just before the two-country border. The bar is on the left-hand side of the road. Dirt and gravel parking lot. Hitching post, too, in case you're horseback.

Inside, ask for Hiram Johnny Walker Quicksilver. Quick. Good chance he'll be there. Drives a Ford 250 with giant dualies. There's a silk screen in the rear window. A red, white, and blue tomahawk. The tomahawk glows in the dark. Can't miss it.

Anyway. Tell him Jesus sent you. Dile que Jesús te envió. Tell him we need to talk. Tell him I got him a job like I said I would. Promised it to him when we was in prison together. (La prisión, dulces recuerdos.) Didn't know what it was at the time, but now I do. Tell him I told him I'd get him a job, trabajo, so I did. The job is waiting just for him. Tell him he'll make so much money he won't have to lift a finger from now on to the end of his days. Not unless he wants to. Tell him to get his ass down here, pronto Tonto. He'll know pronto, Tonto. Money for the plane ticket's in the side pouch of the duffel. Tell him if he drives he can pocket the difference. Doesn't matter. Either way's okay. (He's a cheap ass. Probably will want to drive.)

Tell him to bring an extra pair of cowboy-cut Wranglers (his brand), change of socks, a second pair of Tony Lamas if he wants, but make sure he brings some sneakers ... zapatillas ... some gym shoes for his big ass Injun feet. Might need 'em. Everything's taken care of from there. Need him here by Wednesday, no later than Thursday dusk. Jueves por la noche. Tell him Jesus is calling. Jesús está llamando. Resurrection time. Dead to living. Back to doing the do. He'll know what I'm talking about. Él sabrá. Confía en mí. Trust me.

A day later, me, Hiram Johnny Walker Quicksilver, I'm just standing there at the bar minding my own business. Cowboy hat's rested on the back of my head, casual like, like I like to wear it when I'm relaxing. This dude just walked up out of nowhere and handed me the duffel. He nearly stuffs it in my gut. Thought he might be testing me, you know, duke it out, iitsska, but he just grinned real big. So, I figured it was a good thing. The wad of money was there in the side pouch. All of it. The dude, he pats it, the side pouch, three, four, five times and smiles real wide some more. Points again. Then, the delivery dude, he pats me on the shoulder like we was old pals and turned around and as quickly disappeared. He never said nothing.

The note from Jesus inside the duffel read: Abrazos en bezos, mi amigo. (Hugs & kisses, my friend.)

The crazy, little Mexican had drawn a smiley face next to that with a luscious, prison-naked señorita *next to that.*

For the record, Jesus, he knew. We was prison mates. I pocketed the difference and drove.

CHAPTER 15

Aamsskaapipikani VI
Blackfeet Nation VI

Hiram Johnny Walker Quicksilver sat upright in the chrome chair, the one with the red gingham, oilcloth upholstery. His legs were splayed wide beneath the matching chrome breakfast table. He could've been sitting horseback. The table and chairs, a dinette set, they were a late gift from Esther's sister in Lethbridge. She didn't have the money at the time of the wedding so it took awhile to get it all collected, packaged and delivered in the back of the family pickup.

Hiram, he sipped black coffee. He rubbed his hands and felt carefully for the roping wound the same way he felt for it (and admired it) every morning. The scar moved left to right through his index finger across his knuckle.

Esther sat across from him. She drank her coffee black with a teaspoon of sugar. The white sugar in the open bowl was like a centerpiece. It was spotted with brown coffee stains. Esther stirred hers until the steam quit, then she tasted it again only to start all over. She looked across at Hiram and waited approvingly for his morning insight.

Hiram said to Esther,

When the heist is done, I can finally relax and take a breather. Put my Tony Lamas on the front dash of my F 250 and lean back into the soft vinyl with a cold Woolly Bugger and spit tobacco juice through the space in my front teeth and not give a shit whether it hits the cup or not.

More money than I know what do with. That's what the big man says. Money stashed this high (Hiram lifts his hand above his head) *between the lime and three cartons of toilet paper over by the open pit that we used to use as a crapper ... before the tribe came with the backhoe and cut the thawed ground and set the septic tank ten feet underground and forty, fifty feet from the gravel drive.*

In my good dream, not my bad one, I can smell the fresh horse manure of the six brand new quarter horses I just bought at the tribal auction with the new money. Good horses ... and beautiful. Matsowá' ponokáómitaa. Really good horses. Tapimiim! You know, not broke down and long in the tooth. Ones with shiny coats, long straight legs, and toed properly with the handsome heads of a fine sculpture. Keep 'em in the new corral with a hay manger, either side so they don't kick the shit of one another hogging grain. I make the corral stiff, tight, and pliable out of virgin Aspen timber felled with my sixty-inch Husqvarna.

When I'm done, whenever that is, I can eat flapjacks made with pig lard and government flour in the early morning and drink Canadian whiskey straight from the bottle after eight or nine a.m. till when the sun sets in winter... till ten, even eleven, in summer ... that is if I last that long. Too drunk to know, too drunk to pass out, too drunk to care. It's why you drink. (Hiram Johnny Walker Quicksilver laughs and raises his coffee cup in a toast. Esther raises hers. The cups clink.) *Makes no difference. Actually, I drink whenever I please. After the job, I don't answer to nobody. The probation officer, the warden, the world wide web, not even the tribal council ... they all can kiss my naked ass in a full squat. That is all in my good dream.*

Me and my woman, we are here in the trailer day and night, two fat and lazy Indians belching and farting and belching some more and then slouching in between copulating. That's what will happen. Make no bones about it. And, I will howl like a gray wolf to the open wind I will be so happy.

(Esther raises her cup. Hiram, too. Their cups clink two more times.) Hiram says to Esther:

This, a toast to us, it is when you are too old to lift the gun, and I am too old to duck.

After the big heist, my mother will be proud of her son once again. He made it back to the reservation. She will say that. Back where he belongs. She will say that, too. Back to the double-wide in the evergreen forest in one piece in spite of the nosey and intrusive white man, Napikowann. Custer's white man, that is what she calls them. That is what she would say. She dislikes the white man more than me, but she's a woman so she puts up with things better. Water off a duck's back. You understand.

The white man, Custer's white man, Napikowann, he can kiss my ass, too. Now as well as when I die. That's what I say. I take his money the same way he took our land, nitawahsin-nanni, and left me here to die in between the quaking aspen and the scrub brush with its moose hair dangling like cobwebs in a corner breeze. Screw Custer's white man and the horse he rode in on.

Oh, here, before I forget, let me, Hiram Johnny Walker Quicksilver, digress one time. (Big word 'digress'. Learned that one in prison. White man word for 'go down another path'. This Indian knows all about going down another path. Been in a big, long, drawn-out digress my whole life.)

Anyway.

My life is already too burned up fucking with people that don't matter.

Injun's gotta bitch. Everybody else does. We're the only ones that don't get nothing in the swap.

Esther raised her cup one more time, higher still, and still higher one more time, and smiled proudly. Hiram, too. They touched coffee cups once more, this time like the two were toasting shots and celebrating hardy a rodeo victory in some cavernous and raucous cowboy saloon. True love. Akomimm. Husband and wife. Oom & Ohkiimaan. Hiram and Esther.

Esther, she was a Pawnee from Las Vegas, New Mexico. But, you know that already.

CHAPTER 16

When Jesus Went to Prison
Cuando Jesús Fue a la Cárcel

The Scene:

It was a motel.

The Characters:

There was a woman. Esta mujer.

And, there was the Mexican.

The Narrative:

The real events are herein depicted, say as things really happened.

Then, of course, there were the claims and accusations followed by the denials and disproof. He said. She said.

The two of them, this woman (esta mujer) and Jesus Escobar, stood face to face in the cold air. They easily agreed on everything, a price, outside. The one could see the smoky whiteness of the other's breath as they both looked on (not at one another but away, here and there, and askance) and nodded. It was winter and nighttime.

The *price, it was* next to nothing. He'd thought that at the time and remembered it that way. She'd thought that at the time, too, but she knew that she was desperate for money. They went to the back of the motel. He was on foot. She was on foot.

Seedy, it was the first thought that came to mind when you turned the corner and saw the condition of the place up close, even in the dark. She thought this at first glance because the motel was wrung dry of any semblance to the billboard-worthiness (the one just down the street) as a family accommodation … you know, wholesome, healthy, friendly, with fresh towels and paper-wrapped soap as well as starched bed linens and cute, perfumy pillow mints to match. It was simply the worse for wear.

He thought so too, but he had the key to Room 331. The three numbers together, he remembered them faultlessly in Spanish. He'd stolen the key with the giant green, plastic tag, from a maid's cart in the A.M. She remembered it the same way, too, because he'd boasted to her about what he'd done on their introduction, and at the time she saw no reason for concern and actually saw it as cute or prankish and jejune, even just the roguish other-side of endearing.

They both remembered all of that the same way … that and that the *one* hung crooked at eye level on the front of the door below the peep hole. That and that there were only two floors with a room key in the three hundreds so 331, it made no sense. That and that there was only a straggle of tenants, say ten, maybe twelve people at most which you could tell by the number of cars parked up against the doorway at each of the ground level rooms. All of this was quite obvious and quite easy to recall.

Once past the ice maker, the two walked past the *out of order* sign past the glass cased vending machines, the three side by side, past the *do not disturb* sign and all that was in between, not together but following each other and exchanging the lead along the way.

There was a liquor bottle turned on its flat edge next to an empty, flip top cigarette box on the one cement stair, and up at the start of the second floor, there on the open staircase next to the twisted, green, wrought iron railing was another empty, brown bottle lying label side up the same way. Cheap whiskey. The same brand both places. The same cheap, sickening sweet smell (not like premium whiskey or the way good whiskey smells) both at level one and level two when you walked past just before you made the turn to get to room 331.

He followed her. He gave her the key. She opened the door. Then, he pushed it shut with the heel of his shoe. Neither spoke. They undressed halfway to the lamp light already on over by the desk and the caution-yellow, relic of a telephone sitting on top of the thick telephone book-Bible combo. It was dim and best for both.

Neither showered. She hadn't combed her hair. He never carried a comb. It was all the same as neither made a fuss. *There was nothing between them*, she kept telling herself nervously *so it was really like it wasn't happening* she liked to think. But in fact, it was. Simultaneously, they just slumped onto the bed and began the obligatory, wanton-less groping, the eyes at half-mast (*libido by Braille*, she called it) and the senseless, suspect suspension of all time and space inside a two-bit, sleazy motor court ten by twelve snuggery with pile carpeting so dense, so coarse, and so tall it could have been cut, swathed and baled.

This meeting was by contractual invitation only and an awkward, mismatched dance between rhythm-less beginners, understated and precarious to a fault. You've seen them. Can't keep the beat. Timing is all off and not there. (She was taller than he was.) Embarrassing for everyone around, everyone but them. They don't know, so *they don't know* or see or feel the embarrassment they should. Ignorance, as often as not, really is bliss.

Said he would've or should've kissed her, but she didn't or wouldn't for the same reason. Then, they just lay there on top of the bed covers, finished the body intro, and finally, as naked as two eyeballs under a surgical lamp, started screwing (copulando) in awkward, halfhearted ups and downs while the mattress squeaked and sank, squeaked and sank. It was little more than passionless writhing on his part, but she felt the same way. On this, they both could have or would have agreed had it come up in a post-performance, ten-point customer satisfaction questionnaire.

The bedcovers, of all things, were most noticeable. And, of all things, colored a burnt orange or a crushed gold. (Occupant's call.) The Mexican had his nose pressed into them the whole time so he'd paid no attention and seemed nearly out of breath through most of the formality, *her ordeal* as she named it. *Panting like a dog after an unleashed walk* is what she thought and said to herself almost laughingly during the *do*. Those same bed covers smelled of stale, dried gin or unbranded wine or spilt, Solo cup malt liquor, but it was tough to tell. The bright red Solo cup ... maybe it was a dead giveaway _ she'd noticed it over in the corner, on its side on the floor while they were doing the *dirty*. *Fracking* as she referred to it; that and *fracking* with all *its occupational hazards*. She thought that too, but she dismissed it just as quickly.

This wasn't the time to think *funny* much less blurt out something like that to a paying customer while she was doing her *level best* (the pun, of course she heard the pun; she was the one that had thought it) to conduct business professionally. There was an even much stronger hint of cheap, dryer sheet perfume in the mix, like it was thrown in for good measure to confuse proletariat senses and cover the weeks and months and years of wear and the speckled traces of lurid, other-folks' groveling and unvarnished, disingenuous sex.

She pretended to like what he was doing, but she always said it was hard to *fake rapture*. All *things* considered, *things* seemed to be working for him. She thought that, too.

So, she kept doing whatever it was that he seemed to like the whole time faking her own pre-orgasmic enthusiasm by redoing and reenacting those same things. Things like breathing heavy for effect or passing faint, muffled concupiscent (almost tactical, and most certainly multilingual, in-any-language) instruction into the open air, like a coach from the sideline who, once lost in thought and daydreaming, starts paying attention again only after the full-body collision he just heard in front and nearly on top of him but that he visually had just missed. The two, esta mujer and the Mexican, they were a couple of whistle-less traffic cops working an unattended but suddenly busy intersection.

Then, finally (her thought), there as that burst of movement (his) followed by nothing. She wanted to applaud. *Nothing* was good and her own personal abbreviation for *good riddance.* Joy had arrived. Exuberance couldn't be far behind. Inside, she wanted to cheer. As she always said, she, once again, *had taken one for* the *team.* (Another of her professional, in-the-moment maxims.) Anything, for God's sake, so he would get off, she could get up, collect the rest of her money, and leave.

Just as quickly, that old sixth sense started in. She'd heard it before. It said to her toward the end, '*Told you so.*' Said it like that, the voice in her head did. Kept repeating it over and over and not letting up.

Okay, okay, she wanted to say. Enough already.

But again. '*Told you so*' came back more plainly inside her head at each and every breath. It was that same tone of voice, that brash and unfeeling utterance, that callous and distasteful inflection speaking out from her psyche each time like she hadn't heard it before or the first time.

'*Told you you were going to be sorry,*' said the bully side of her inner voice.

It was a caw. A mockingbird's cant. And, she could already feel what was coming and on the way. The shock, the disappointment not to mention the lousy, stinking shame and regret once the *double cross* had actually settled in. But, she didn't want to admit it or face it or hear it fully, at least not right now, not right then and there anyway because, again, she really, really needed the money. (Oh, God how she needed the money.) She dreaded it so if this whole entire thing was honestly going to come to pass as another unpaid and luckless day.

Chalk up another one to experience, said the voice.

Oh, go away, she said almost aloud.

She had an oracle's gift or an intuitive yet surly and unwanted talent in foretelling gloom, the grievous, the baleful, moreover, the failed side of living as well. It was like a sensor, not as loud as a siren, and always too late in the experience to save her like some ship's beacon off a rocky barrier from her own pitiless peril and torrential doom.

Knowing it was one thing, experiencing it another, and yet always it was painful and always it still hurt, as each time it seemed to penetrate into some other deeper, darker, and untouched corner of her soul like a pin prick or dull scalpel on a young child's unblemished skin.

She saw it for what it was, dour and jaded, and worse, it was perversity set on its own sharp and prickly edge, and always it seemed to be spread out like a cast net against her. She knew this about herself and the way things broke. She was the canary; she was the mine. *Watching out loud* is what she called it, so she sat very still and listened as this man, the Mexican, spoke up in a faint, disjointed, and unpunctuated voice.

Said he *didn't have the money*.

Said he'd send it to her when he *got a job*.

Said *it* (the sex) was *okay*, but *not great*. No es genial. She could've done more. Been better.

Titillation. Not what he said, but what she thought she heard him infer. He stood there with his hands on his hips, his trousers mostly on but not latched, with his shirt off. Played the part, you know, *the role* or the *role-playing* thing. For a moment, he did it well. You know. The dissatisfied customer, with stranger to stranger psychological detachment, the subtle numbness, the vibe he picked up from her and her lack of cheap-motel-sex sensitivity.

Something? "*Alguna cosa*," is what he said. "*Algo*," too. He said it in Spanish, she remembered that, and somehow and for some unknown reason she knew what he meant. And then, he said it again, "*Alguna cosa*?" And, then, "*Algo es el problema*," or as she interpreted it "something is the problem," like he was puzzled. But what? she thought. Maybe he was trying to express himself concerning a real and tangible issue that she or he each in his own inept way didn't understand, but more than likely she thought as quickly and instinctively, he was probably just reaching for the con. That's what she surmised; it came with the territory, this profession of hers, so giving him the *benefit of the doubt wasn't* okay after all, and the doubt washed away any benefit she might possibly have earlier or momentarily conceded. His English was lousy, brittle even, or, as likely and for other nefarious reasons, brusque and contrived.

"*Been there*," he said next as she just sat there taking it all in. She was befuddled to say the least. *Been there* ... whatever that meant? she thought in a second stare.

Could've done this, should've done that. (The list grew.) And then, he said *he was* "*leaving*." She was sure she heard that correctly. It needed no translation. He said it so plainly, so conclusively, and with such precision it was like the snap of a dry twig in a silent forest.

"*Outta here*," he blurted. "*Gone*." (Him and his Mexicali brogue.) "*Mas tarde. Ido. Places to go, people to meet*," he infused. "*Outta here, skank*."

He said that after he stood up from lacing his shoes. He picked up his jacket and began to put it on only to pause as he heard her suddenly erupt.

"What?" she said. Said it in a shrill protest, as *Evocative's* first cousin (the unnamed and undesignated muse) and, what's more, in the masculine gender.

He said he gave her what he had. Then, like a peace offering, he placed both hands open and exposed in front of her and in perfectly plain and literate English called it *a down payment*.

"Down payment, my ass!" she said as she stood up almost violently.

She called him a *sorry* fuck *wad, a two-bit scumbag, a fucking little, no account Mexican bitch! With a puny little Mexican dick!* Waved her hands about in the air (enraged) showy like a symphony conductor. Captured the penis thing, the size, on one crass throw, more a flick, off the last knuckle of her pinky nail. *That small!* is what it said. Even t*inier than that!* She didn't need to repeat herself. Her look said it all, even made it worse.

Jesus coolly, summarily, seamlessly reached into his pocket feeling for the smooth edge of the blade. He drew it across the meat of his thumb. He flicked the cover open. The razor thin box cutter still hidden, he looked up, away, and right, and, then, off into space (ceiling tiles streaked with brown stains) staring at nothing, pensive-like, real casual, into the other corner of the room, sort of like he was calculating a large figure from a multiple-choice question, drew the sharp cutter from his trouser pocket, turned back, and slit her face. Just like that. Cross ways. Fast.

Faster even than that, she was bleeding badly from the cut wound when he left motel room 331 and the second floor, while she stood there still and motionless, holding her face and the cup and saucer full of red blood now in the palm of her hand. She hadn't yet begun to cry or whimper or wail it had happened so immediately, instantly, and with such flagrant and unsympathetic speed.

Jesus Escobar didn't look back. He began to run when he got past the open, ground-floor stairwell at the end of the broken concrete.

What the hell, he thought running. (He always say that, said his Mexican running buddies quoting Jesús Ángel Escobar, el gángster, in their own broken dialect. That's what he always say to himself when he finds himself in a pinch, in a bind, en un lazo.)

What the hell, you fuckin' gabacho whore. What you doin' fuckin' a Mexican anyway, cunt? called out Jesus Escobar in a hollow breath.

"Reconquista," he shouted back into the night air because he always felt bravest when he was in a getaway and there was no one else around. He disappeared between two parked cars as it was nighttime.

But, in one of the cars, a dated, earlier model pickup with a cursive smattering etched into the glass all the way around, sat a lone woman, a suspicious woman, dialing numbers on her phone and calling out.

From there, what was done was done.

Later by an hour.

This woman, esta mujer, she stepped forward through the glass door. She sat quietly in the chair offered to her and drew another deeper breath so that she could think more clearly and piece together the words that she needed to say. She was there to tell her story and express her dismay and disappointment in what fate had scripted or let happen to her.

The two men at the police station, one behind a desk, listened with the stolid pretense of interest and concern.

She was alone. Half covered in a short blanket, she held the ice inside the hand towel against the side of her face. The towel was bloody. As wet as it was, the leftover melt dripped seamless, red spots onto her soiled trousers, past her wrinkled t shirt and her bleached and ratted hair. All told, the ice and the towel kept the damage contained. Her eye had swollen nearly shut, but she could see well enough to recognize the late-night hour on the clock on the far wall behind the one man's right shoulder as well as the faces just below that in the framed picture. It had to have been his wife, a daughter and a son. The three smiled in unison back at her while he looked back across his desk at her; his tie and collar had been loosened from a long day.

She could feel the swelling moving into her upper lip as she spoke. Her face hurt, but the cold made it hurt less. She wanted to see a doctor, she said, but only after she got this off her chest. She apologized three times for looking like such a mess but continued to talk and tell her side of the story. It was important that the man that had done this to her be caught. It was more important that he go to jail.

"It wasn't right what he did," she said plainly.

"It just wasn't right," she said. Her good eye lit up expressive-like after she'd said it better and more audibly the second time because the first time the swelling got in the way.

And, "*Uncalled for*," she said. She repeated the same theme backtracking over and over in the same or similar words to the two men both of them looking at her from behind the one man's desk like saying it and them listening to it would undo her arrangement with the Mexican, correct the mistake, patch the slash wound on her face, mend her obtuse frailty, and nab the money she was due as a consequence and requiem for her haggard emotion. And, all of this at the same time.

She continued on for another half hour.

Two hours and thirteen minutes had passed.

Seemingly out of thin air, there were two patrol cars hovering about the small area and apparently both were looking for the same thing. Both were equipped with double twin-lamp head gear and a single search lamp the size of a small hog. Together, they quickly circled their suspect (the Mexican, Jesús Ángel Escobar) in a nearby vacant lot. That same suspect had managed to casually embosk himself in a clump of tall bent grass between a stash of dried leaves, downed brush, and a small, disheveled rick of straw.

At first, he had been a shadowy figure ducking skittishly between a block and mortar laundromat side entrance and a small, abandoned filling station. The tall dispenser casings in the covered service island, one beside the other, made for decent cover. The pump handles on the end of the stiff, black rubber hoses were still attached, but all four were sprawled out like dead bodies on a cold, cracked cement slab.

Across the way, Jesus played possum and pretended not to breathe.

The taller, leaner deputy of the two in the short, heavy waist jacket shined the handheld lantern straight away into the man's eyes, the man lying on the ground, and said, "Boy, what are you doing lying there playing possum?"

Jesus couldn't see anything past the silhouette and halo of the bright light. No faces. Two voices. Couldn't decipher the words over the car engines much less their figures, shapes, or silhouettes. But, in another moment he could make out the county emblems on the two vehicles with the roof blue signal lamps which were now swirling in flickers, spurts, sputters, glints and sparks the way enforcement blue always looks. Jesus had been here before. *Situación similar.*

He was caught. He knew it. And, he knew why. The deputies handcuffed him and hauled him into the county jail. There, he was booked and his likeness photographed.

"Jesús Án'hell Escobar, says here … With a rap sheet long enough to fill a cookbook," said the first deputy as he secured the new prisoner's jail cell door.

"Jesús Án'hell Escobar, in you go, partner," said the second deputy holding high the evidentiary plastic bag with the box cutter. "With a woman's blood stains still on your trousers and your fingerprints all over the box cutter that you used to commit the heinous crime. What a shame," said the same man turning about to walk away.

The Mexican, he was guilty as charged with no way out.

Three years and seven months had gone by.

When Jesús Ángel Escobar reminisced, he would tell his story and say casually (casualmente), chivalrously, "She was a whore. We bartered. Vendimos. I paid for her services. Pagué por sus servicios. Where I come from (de donde vengo), that is what we do. No questions asked."

Cuervo, a Jesus camello, pistolero, contrabandista, fellow inmate, and amigo, he listened while the two played cards, a game of twenty-one, at empty, prison cafeteria table # four. The ante was three cigarettes to start.

Jesus continued.

"She became angry (se enojó) and tried to strike me due to my *increíble* prowess, my virility, and stamina in the mount, so I defended myself," said Jesus.

He lite another cigarette before he had finished the one that he had going and then dealt another hand, flat footed and hunched over as if displeased. His machismo never blurred in the recall.

"Regardless of her charges and her accusations, little more than make-believe and *histeria*, I am still today an innocent man. El hombre inocente, amigo. You are speaking with him now, Cuervo. That is all that I have to say."

There were now two trails of entwined smoke from cigarillo one and cigarillo two in the tin cup ash tray as the two men studied their cards.

"And, look at me," Jesus continued. "After all this time, I am still the lone prisoner of this one manipulative harlot, a whore by trade. Me, a guiltless man. Wrongly accused, incarcerated for certain, yet for crimes I did not commit. Let it be known far and wide, that I, Jesús Ángel Escobar, have been jailed for all this time because of this one woman's lies, the color of my skin, and my national origin. All of this, it is the same verdict and for this I sit here today staring out from behind this cage that some men, funcionarios each and every one, call their prison. It is true what I speak, amigo. Es cierto."

Voices within were known to echo so the two men kept their voices low. Jesus threw an eight to the ten showing, and again, it was another win for him. He stuffed one more Cuervo cigarette behind his left ear to match the one behind his right which further complimented his winnings of Cuervo cigarillos laid out neatly in front of him on the table in a small pile.

"She was an emaciated slut," resumed Jesus. He inhaled from cigarillo #2 then exhaled and placed cigarillo #2 back at the edge of the tin cup. "La puta, esta mujer, she was drug infested, with hair the texture of a weathered bird's nest and bleached to match her parched guera complexion. Her collar bone stuck out even from behind the fall of her t shirt … Guns N'Roses … their silly faces across her flat chest. I remember this like it was yesterday. And for this I would risk my life? Mi vida? No, mi amigo. It would be ridiculous to even think such a thought much less to act on it knowing full well the dire consecuencias. Absurdo, el listillo. You are a smart man, Cuervo, and you know that a man of my intelligence and talent would never do something so preposterous and so estúpido that I would put myself at risk forever and wind up in a place like this."

Cuervo said little, gestured less, and listened passively only to study his cards hoping for a change of luck in the next hand. He was down two and one-half packs with only a half a pack remaining.

CHAPTER 17

The Spirits in Prison

1 Peter 3:19

Jesus went and preached to the spirits in prison.

W*hen we were in prison ...*
Jesus, he would stand in front of this skinny little mirror and look at himself for a long time. I would see him do this when I passed his cell. He would wrestle his biceps into a knot. He would suck in his stomach. He would try and flex his little, baby flab tits and squeeze his neck into a bow to try and make everything bigger. Sometimes I would stand out in the hallway looking in just to see if he'd notice me. He never did. He never flinched. Didn't know I was there. He would grin wide and then squeeze his face into a frown or a big scowl, like he was some kind of badass. I guess in his own way he was. Not much of him, but he was dangerous enough. Said he liked Satan, whatever that meant. Said they were soulmates and brothers in arms. Talked to the mirror. Said, "I am a man without a conscience." (He would then snarl almost like a rabid dog.) Then, he'd say, "There are not many of us, but I am one." More Jesus-talk to make himself look big my guess.

Jesus, he was shorter than a handshake, slighter than a smile, but he was who he was.

He was a sight standing there in his little inmate briefs, his chest all poked out, his back straightened to attention right before he'd have to exhale. Next to the black and blue skull & crossbones stamped on the top side of his nipple was a tattoo in scarlet letters, Pablo Es Primo. The letters were laced in a black vortex. That's what Jesus called it, black vortex. In the next block of lettering to the left of his right nipple was some homemade, prison copperplate script, Ser Hombre, Muy, Muy Cuidadoso, followed by, I Take Mother Fucker to Another Level. Jesus claimed Pablo Escobar, the drug kingpin, was his first cousin once removed. Claimed him as another soulmate as well. You know, the big fraternity of badasses, at least in Jesus' mind. On his other bicep was the raised relief of El Chapo himself. Underneath, Yo era un maldito enfermo desde el principio! (I was a sick fuck from the start.) You deal with it. Below that, Jesús Is Lord! Jesús es el Señor! It was inside the banner scroll at the top of his right shoulder. Then, there was the imprint of one Pablo hippopotamus, from the famous herd of hippos at Hacienda Nápoles, just at the base of his skull. Another tribute to the man.

Stenciled just above his pubic line was a colorfully dressed and mustached Jesús Malverde. "Who better to watch over my machinery (mi pene y mis bolas, my pecker and my balls, amigo) than the patron saint of narcos," said Jesús Ángel Escobar, all smiles. When Jesus was only partially clothed, the top portion of the perfectly coiffed man's portrait appeared ever so slightly above the waistband of his prison briefs like a ventriloquist's dummy peeking half way out from his carrying case.

On his back side, Santa Muerte stretched from the top of both shoulders to the crack of his ass. Nuestra Señora, she gleamed. Black where her eyes used to be. The yellow, hollowed outline of her features. The smile as such, all behind the dead woman's scowl, a witch's cackle as leftover, wrapped in a crown of beads and silken scarfs and armed with a hangman's scythe. I have to admit it was pretty spooky to catch Jesus shirtless from behind. He was a year-round trick or treat silhouette, and nobody laughed.

I seen shit in the marines but nothing like Jesus. He was head to toe one big walking, talking, ink soaked, fuck-you-and-the-horse-you-rode-in-on poster board. He liked it that way. He was drunk on his own disease. Known others like that. Lots of them in prison. And they all wonder how they got there.

On other days, I'd hear him in his cell chatting away. No one was there. He was in his cell. I was in mine. Both of us alone.

Asked him once, Bro', who you talking to in the middle of the night?

God, he'd say. Dios, amigo.

God? I'd say.

Yeah, God, he'd say.

Man, I'd say, that's some pretty irreverent trash to be talking to God.

Yeah, he'd say back.

And that was it. I let it go. Two convicts talking shit and one of 'em talking to God. Pretty sure Jesus thought he was connected to the big guy in charge. You know, the name and all. God complex, maybe. Don't know. Told him so. He just laughed. Little man complex, maybe. Don't know. Maybe both is the same thing. The truth is, the truth always gets truer the more you stare at it.

Jesus, he was always kind of the other side of the shadow. We got along, but he was.

Sometimes, Jesus would stand in his cell and yell through the bars, "Hey, America! You listening? Estás escuchando?" That's what he would say. "Hey, remember me?" he would say. "Well, guess what, gringo nation? Yeah, it's me, Jesus. Jesús Ángel Reconquista Escobar. And I'm back. After all this time living in this hell hole, I'm back. He vuelto. I'm fucking back and badder than ever, America. Malo que nunca. Malo que nunca."

I figure some days even the devil must sit back and admire Jesus he was so crazy.

Jesus, that one time, he let out a scream so loud it made my toes curl, woke the warden, probably the dead, and sounded the alarm. Jesus, he just laughed and beat on his little chest and kept hollering, "Check me out, America before I check you out, or before I check out altogether. Me, the freebooter from south of the border. Hola, amigo. Jesús resucitó. Jesus is resurrected. Roll away the stone, mother fucker. Ruede lejos la piedra, hijo de puta. Roll away the stone."

My business partner and one crazy, fucking Mexican.

(I never did try to talk to God when I was in prison. Figured if He'd been listening beforehand, I wouldn't be there.)

CHAPTER 18

The Crucifixion of Jesus
By
Jesús Ángel Escobar

When you looked closer ... stepping up and holding the canvas (like it was framed) at arm's length ... you could see before you three complete figures. Those same three figures were encircled closely (almost wrapped) in a dark, ominous setting ... black, low-lying clouds, lit but faint, apparent yet purposely gray and dreary. In the distant backdrop, centurions stood roguelike, arms folded. They were draped in red cloaks against a backdrop of another smaller circle of servile figures, mourners say, at the foot of a tall wooden piling crossed ever so slightly but unlike what you have imagined or been instructed to think or pictured in your mind's eye. The servile figures, call them mourners, they sat about like Dachau leftovers on a train rail awaiting, wistfully, some final freedom. They were speechless, yet settled, nestled, yet cornered. One man's legs were crossed. Another woman's baleful stare appeared almost simpleminded in its stupefaction ... her own utter disbelief. Self absorbed most certainly, yet disbelief is always self absorbed. At the same time, the woman kneeled somehow comfortably and content in a leeward crouch facing the tall wooden piling, now empty. There was no longer a man hanging there ... no longer suspended. He had been taken down as dead.

There was a soft glint of sunlight from the heavens cast downward. There were golden threads through the mist of dew and breaking dawn as well. Black-gray clouds bisected the central figure standing before the others. Not a tall man yet his posture made him look so ... there with his head up, his shoulders back, his feet planted firmly, his arms by his side in a natural drape. Most apparent were his eyes. They were aglow with a peculiar but certain relief ... as if to say ... *the ordeal is finally over, and, now, I'm on the other side. Besides*, his expression seemed to say, w*asn't it or isn't it always about getting, finally, to the other side?* There were probably other subliminal messages in these eyes of his ... his stance, too, his calm, as well, but the eyes had it. They were brightness and light amidst the gloom.

Besides, how could anyone be deified for such an obvious (a clinical case), overwrought, and overabundant self-effacement?

Across the rest of the picture from the top right-hand section of the canvas down, the setting achieved a majesty. The spontaneous precision left the painting beautifully if not unevenly and inexplicably parsed by anyone at whatever level. Some might even tag the work as stunningly incomprehensible or mysterious or moving and all of this without pretense. However, it could only leave you, the viewer, vulnerable, perhaps winded, or even capsized by the angst and eeriness you might feel once you learned of the artist's blood stench, the unholy madman as draftsman ... least it be some kind of a trick as Satanic horseplay.

The painting was signed Jesús Ángel Escobar in a swirly long hand in the same color as the man's eyes, the man who was that same painting's central figure.

CHAPTER 19

The Third Cell Down on The Right

Letters from prison.

Habib wrote these words. (He was Habib Alif Ali-Ali, inmate C-128483. Everyone asks ... Ali-Ali ... What's with the hyphen?... Answer, he invariably would explain. Once for the prophet Mohammed's son in law, once for the pugilist-prizefighter. His cell was three down from Hiram's. He was next door to Jesus on the right along the hollow corridor.)

His letter read:

Ahabk. Ahabk. Ahabk.

My dearest Myrna,

I have dreamed of you. I have dreamed of you night and day. I have dreamed of us. We are two star-crossed souls. Yet, this is no accident. Our love is meant to be. Of this, I am certain. When I saw your face for the first time, I knew we would be lovers and friends and soulmates for all eternity. Heaven is a state of mind perhaps, but love has no boundaries, no hopelessness. I will wait for you. I will wait for you here. Be kind to yourself. Ignore those others there that want you. They are carnally intentioned only. A vice unto itself. My motive is to have you near to me forever and the two of us enraptured for all time. Kisses from the devil's own den. Soon I will be set free. It is almost tomorrow, then the next day and a week. Soon I am yours. Habib, Your Lover and Allah's servant awaiting my release. Alla azim.

It was the third letter of four so far that week. He would fold each one with deliberateness (servile gallantry more than not) and painstaking care. It was, by now, surely more ritual than habit. He slid each handcrafted missive into the next prison-issue envelope and dropped them one by one into the *Outgoing* mail slot on the first floor on his way to evening mess. He reread each one six or eight times to check his punctuation, particularly his spelling, before kissing the glue gum as he sealed the sleeve. He only hoped that Myrna read them. He hoped much more than that that she saved herself for him in his absence.

Purity's pure, wrote Habib. *Celibacy, it's truest companion ... it's best friend. Abstinence makes the heart grow fonder. Myrna, remember this always as you think of me. Ahabk. Ahabk. Koblh. Your devoted messenger. Habib.*

The third cell past the stairwell (Habib's) was made particularly noisy by its proximity to the world-within. Guards, prisoners, custodians, more prisoners, more guards, another trail of custodians and parade of inspectors, it was the thoroughfare of incarceration's folly.

Five times a day, the words, the Habib verbiage rang out like a strident, cockeyed East Indian chant from a hollow Turkish bath. Tile accented, no less. It was a mystical rambling complete with inutterable diphthongs, paired beside thin-strung sitars and twin tawdry tablas, that bray in the offing. All of it was little more than an accompanying distraction to the clutter of sordid, filthy language and disheveled, cumbersome movement all about in cell block seven.

But, for Habib, it was tolerable. He was the silent type. He shared little, he asked for less. He sat for long hours with his back straight, his head bowed, his vision limp and languid, his legs crossed. It was a kneeling position the common convict would petition against and label libelous torture. The unwonted posture gave way to sessional chants and unintelligible prayers as well as the ups and downs of a small boat tipping back and forth, uncharted, in an indifferent open sea. Habib, he was the mystic in our midst. Squatting there, Habib was more the mere lunatic than those amongst the unquieted rabble.

He had never conformed to prison swearing, or so it seemed. He eluded prison jive-as-conversation except as it pertained to himself and then only in private, then only about the others, the non-believers, when alone and only when *his* thoughts could be disguised as liturgy, a cloaked liturgy most deeply if only symbolically ensconced in a self-absorbed supremacy and *his* inner circle of *his own* hereafter.

Habib was a living testament to a fatwa gone wrong.

CHAPTER 20

Naatowá'pínaa
Holy Man from the Cave of Hira

He said that he was a holy man. He was, after all, Habib Alif Ali-Ali, and, he proclaimed that he was Canada's Holy Man, the one and only true Holy Man. He was on fire. He stood inside his cell and recited his vision. Each time he said these words, this vision, this personal interpretation of his own religion's transience, gave him new life and hope for another different day, like it was fresh breath against the orange glow and dying embers of his beleaguered plight and his fading delusion. That is what he told me. When he spoke those words from inside his prison cell, he laid his hands open as proof like he was gathering sunlight or testing a cloudless sky for snowflakes yet to fall. The glimmer in his eye spoke to that same truth, or so he would have liked for you to think.

None before him, he said, and there would be none after. He said that, too.

He said that he had been lifted from the Cave of Hira over a fortnight during a lengthy and arduous fast after a deep and repentant trance-like and cataleptic meditation, one that only God could have sanctioned and ordained. He was as sure of that as well and said so to insure himself of what he claimed.

He was certain that he had been transported here (to Alberta) by Mohammed with the divine and intrepid intervention of Allah Himself. Allah beckoned, he said.

Canada was Mecca anew, Mecca's future in this the new dawn, pre-dawn he called it, the true future of Islam. Allah's destiny, that is what he called it. Of this, he was so certain that he had staked his claim, his life on the outcome and cast his fate into the hands of his God like a man in small boat and the thunderous waterfall in plain view before him.

He prayed ten times a day. Sometimes twelve. Even fourteen on religious holidays and his days off, and claimed the scripture's instruction was insufficient, benign, ineffectively limp if not brazenly impotent in the undertaking. As he saw it, for Allah to overtake the World and see righteousness conquer evil and the unholy, prayers and prayers alone simply would not do. Islam's ultimate victory, the capitulation and subjugation of infidels one and all, must come by way of the sword, of a most forceful jihad, so that in the end the spoken word of Allah was of little or secondary consequence. Triumph was at hand (and by the hand), and all that mattered.

Me, Hiram Johnny Walker Quicksilver, the Blackfoot warrior, I listened to all this and more, and on more than one occasion. Each time, I nodded for sure, like I had not heard these words and sayings the first time … or the other times. So, yes, I played along. It is prison. Too, I said to myself, it was Habib. Another god-boy talking here, kemosahbee. What they can't convince themselves of? The journey only ends when they are gone. Bull rushes to bull shit and back. It don't never stop. Wise old Blackfeet chief says … *Listen, or your tongue will make you deaf.*

CHAPTER 21

The Fatwa
&
Hobby Goes to Jail

Habib Alif Ali-Ali entered quietly through a side door and took a sit in the dimly lit far corner. He pulled up his chair in an underhanded second tug and patiently waited for whatever it was that was to come. Directly across from him was the fully lit, floor-to-ceiling mural of a leggy and buxom exotic (belly) dancer, tagged properly or improperly as *Adira Baraka*. Yes, nearly Abracadabra but not. This appealing portrait, a cleverly enticing and erotic likeness for certain, was a very close knockoff of the real deal, the Flemish Euro-dancer by way of Khartoum who had performed for the group three years running on alternate holidays and special occasions such as the irregular bachelor party or the boy-to-man celebration on the tail of Ramadan and always to the coterie's delight. Discerningly, Habib admired the mural woman ... her sumptuous curves, her mouthwatering posture, her suggestive and prurient pose, her tantalizingly sheer (it was azure chiffon) and strategically-placed costume-cover... from over on his side of the room because the painting was that lifelike.

In the premeeting, there was banter all about, mostly loose and whimsical, however, Habib showed little interest by keeping to himself and, when spoken to, keeping his voice almost as low as his profile. Not even the lightly provocative chatter gave him cause for concern. Habib had merely complied with an inside directive and, as one of a dozen or more sanctioned team players, had made his appearance.

This coven of believers, they were sacrosanct, robed, bearded, sparsely shaven to shaggy, sandals in the chill of winter, buddy-buddy and smiles all round. A shisha here, a chillum there, it left a smoke-filled haze hovering throughout the room up above the taqiyahs and kufiyas into the corners and recesses of the cellar floor ceiling. A short and stocky-built, God-fearing group, they were a Quran's crew (all hail and all hands on deck!), jihadist, self-proclaimed, adamant each and every one. As likely but unprofessed, they were little more than a feral clowder of stragglers, calicos and tabby-strays, striped and solids, each one unalike and individually misintended, coiffed only by measure of their self-indulgent sanctity and back-stabbing malefaction.

Their leader motioned them closer, a *lend me your ear* gesture, so they gathered even closer together like packed subway soma motionless and soulless, inbound at rush hour on an unnumbered commuter car. His directive was more mullah garnished-and-peppered intended to gerrymander these, his band of religious gypsies, away from their own dull and meaningless sense of themselves (their measly, pathetic little lives, he'd called it) and steer them to his primeval, premeditated, and misplaced purpose. Not a lesser Caesar, an apologetic Anthony, or nominally brooding Brutus among them, but, still, they were all present and accounted for, front and center. Team huddle was now in session.

Imani Kahn, the spiritual guide and leader savant, stood in the middle. He rested an elbow on one knee and his foot atop the lone wooden stool in the cold belly of the blackguard's den. Pose struck, he was the thinker. Alternately, he was Patton before a battle's dawn. Too, he was the ferryman, this his river Styx, these his (Charon's) souls, and so his defining glint was in turn his defining moment.

"This guy walks into the bar," began Imani Khan. A joke to lighten the mood. Always, experience told him, a warmup served one best. "The guy says to the bartender, *I'll have a Tanqueray and tonic.*"

"This same guy, the one that has just walked into the bar and ordered the Tanqueray and tonic, he sees this little, little man," said Imani Kahn holding his hands horizontal and parallel to one another to accentuate the diminutive stature of the little man in his joke. "This little man, he is, say, twelve, or maybe fourteen inches in height. Only this tall. And this little man, he is at the other end of the bar playing a very tiny piano. And, the little man, he is quite the piano player. Such beautiful music all about.

The guy that has just walked in at the other end of the bar points with his index finger and says to the bartender, 'The piano player? *What's up? Where did he come from?*'

Imani Kahn looked back into the eyes of Habib … his best Bela Lugosi … with his most competitive and sarcastic smile, one that he felt was particularly forceful, subtle yet fierce. *You know and I know, so we both know all things that are between Muslim brothers* is what his smile said in a figurative yet block-lettered and bold insinuation. Of course, his message was subliminal but opportunistically transposed and meant to be sucked up by his victim like a bank note through some holy pneumatic chute. Imani Kahn stared a second time across and deeper into the eyes of Habib for his own reasons, reasons as yet to be revealed to the unsuspecting sycophant, Habib Alif Ali-Ali.

In an aside, Imani Kahn said, "This joke is the best that I have for you today, Habib. Enjoy, my brother." It was confidential, however more predator to prey.

Habib smiled back unwittingly as one so-called friend to another.

Imani Kahn continued his joke.

"The bartender replies to the customer, '*There is a genie in the Men's Room who grants wishes. Any wish you want, the genie makes the wish come true. One nod of his head and Presto! Your wish is granted just like that.*' The bartender snaps his finger.

So, the guy that has just walked in puts down the Tanqueray and tonic and as quickly runs to the Men's Room saying, '*This I got to see.*'

Sure enough, my brothers, there in the Men's room is the genie standing in the corner of the Men's room. He is tall, his arms folded, his genie hat on his head just so, with the serious demeanor like the genies of old, the ones that always used to grant the wishes without question. So, this genie says to the man, 'Sahib, *your one wish is my command. Say the words, and it will come to pass.*'

So, this guy just as quickly blurts out, '*Okay, I wish for a million bucks!*'

As quickly, the genie nods, and the whole entire room fills with a puff of smoke followed by a room full of ducks and wall-to-wall quacking, flapping, waddling, squawking, fluttering, honking, nesting, fighting, pecking, and biting. Ducks everywhere. The guy from the bar forges his way through the feathers and webbed feet, the duck bills, and dirty looks until he is back out of the Men's Room into the open bar where he had started and where it all began.

The man brushes another dozen or more feathers from his lapel and looks at the bartender and says, '*I think your genie is a bit hard of hearing.*'

'*So, what did you wish for?*' asks the bartender.

'*I wished for a million bucks,*' replies the guy at the bar, 'and got *a million ducks.*'

To which the bartender replies: 'So, do *you think that I actually wished for a twelve-inch pianist?*'

Everyone all around in their matching dishdashas broke into a most uproarious laughter. In the mix was uncloseted applause and delirious backslapping, even simultaneous and irreverent

Western high-fives, not to mention the preemptive Islamic waggles and gesticulations. Even Habib, who laughed loudest, slapped Imani Kahn on the back … comradery's step child or sibling to an awkward acquaintance … but as quickly caught himself thinking and speaking aloud to himself, *not much there under the swell and fluff of your Taliban cloak, oh great emir, Imani Kahn.* Particularly (Habib thought) considering all the posturing, bluster, and big talk.

What a punchline! exclaimed one brother in cryptic Sudanese, bent double with his hand on a double cloaked knee.

Funniest thing I ever heard, replied another in southside Yemeni, laughing out loud showing his golden canine in a furtive glint and gleam.

Not since the first twelve minutes of the Six-Day War had everyone laughed so boisterously, raucously, and with such an apprehensive and edgy glee. Hard to believe I know, but true. Belly laughs all round. Cavorting. Snorting. Knee slapping with impish cartoon figures dancing in each and one another's heads. *Oh, how funny are these jokes of cell leader, Imani Kahn!* all their faces seemed to say.

"So, what do you think?" asked Imani Kahn in a disingenuously unselfish misgiving.

"Funny mo' fo', huh?" replied Imani Kahn answering himself self-assuredly as the others nodded like bobble heads on a spring-loaded dash. For reasons of his own, Imani Kahn stayed mainly focused on Habib though Habib hadn't yet felt the visual peel.

"Plus, I just love the term *mo' fo!*," said Imani Kahn. "Quite the American phrase, do you not think?"

He paused, deep in Mullah (manipulation) pseudo-thought, then continued unabated even within the irreverently boisterous chatter and laughter and cognitive smiles all about him.

"*Mo' fo*," continued Imani Kahn, "as explained … *the American mother who works at this fire station and drives this firetruck* and is so called the *mother trucker*! How ingenious are these Americans, sometimes! They rhyme almost as much as they mate *the mother* and *the trucker* somehow in a seamless translation blend into different words altogether that are unrecognizable to the outside world. Nowhere in our Arabic language much less Arabic custom would this woman be allowed into this fire station much less work there. And then, to drive the truck! Is too funny. Or, mate the mother with the machine (the truck)! Ha ha, hahaha! Preposterous! Still, too funny for words in any language once again. As the master sleuth Shermlock Holmes once said, *What one man can invent another can discover!*"

The raucous, strident laughter ratcheted up to what could only be described as good old pork-fed, Americanized back slapping, swollen bellies and all. Almost in unison, their ghutras and igals nearly capsized in the moment the scene became so boisterous and disorderly, but each man caught his headgear in a side step before it fell off and ruined the gaiety and merrymaking.

Imani Kahn stepped back and respired heavily once more. In another instant, he looked away in a different direction altogether. Theatrically, he stared faintly into the great beyond … even if in actuality it was only the tattered and stained, cobwebbed ceiling above him. And then, meditatively, he fixed his vision on the great beyond and its vast unknown … if only the far side of his eyelids which remained tightly shut in this, his momentary, self-engrossed personal abstraction.

He exhaled once more audibly which, for his purposes, accentuated his own religious force as some greater, out-of-body experience where in fact he or his charade was little more than an enfeebled, old spinster poignantly and reminiscently rummaging through a vast, cobwebbed attic full of tired and useless junk. On another inhale, he imagined Allah, his Allah, that same Allah that had surely endowed the sweep of air in and through and circulating about his lungs as if it most certainly was there to champion the greater cause of all things Imani-Islam. Metaphor upon metaphor, religious simile to secular smile, it all bubbled up and cogitated and breathed even greater life into this movement of his, for their quiet-frenzied and fanatical fate was now at his behest, and his delight since hope and conquest was most assuredly at hand as the ultimate and final goal.

With undaunted purpose inside his scheme, he began again.

"But, now we come to the most important topic of the day, my fellow comrades, for it is no joking matter. But, I must confess to you, my brother Habib, that this is *your mission* and not so much with the humor and silliness with which I began. Jocularity so often begets sobriety. Yet, it makes the truth of reality and its higher purpose easier to swallow and digest."

Imani Khan paused and, with his eyes closed more devoutly than before, drew in a deeper breath for all the world to witness.

"Today, I, Imani Khan, grand apostle of Allah and second disciple of Mohammed, give you, Habib Alif Ali-Ali,

First ... your suicide mission.

Second ... your vestal virgins as promised and as partial reward.

And, lastly ... behind our own pearly gates, the golden paved streets of Mecca's own heaven as the hereafter.

As we all here know, none of these things can be taken lightly as they must be earned and are all a gift from on high."

Imani Kahn stepped to a long table beside the opposite, windowless wall and opened a folded cloth one corner at a time. Such subtle deftness, such histrionic and heartfelt care, such subdued and underhanded resolve, it could have only been replicated by the hand of Iago himself.

Plastic explosives, one whispered to Habib.

Oh, really? said Habib nonchalantly but only in a nod and a mime.

For you, Habib, the next nearest one to him muttered.

Oh? replied Habib as confused and dumbfounded as before.

Yes, said another excitedly.

Me? shadowed Habib in response.

Yes, you, the three nearest nodded in unison. *It is a fine day for holy martyrdom, Habib. Praise be to Allah. And, praise be to you, mujahid Habib.*

A day later, in the pre-dawn hours, Habib Alif Ali-Ali sat alone on a worn, wooden subway bench. He was bound by a railyard's worth of double tracked plastic explosives, fuses, and a lone igniter. His crotch bore the brunt of the double-cross affixed to his chest. The wrap stretched longitudinally sternum to thigh to leg hinge and back again. As it was, everything beneath his Arabic getup and garb was most uncomfortable from the lopsided, genital-binding snare of the Taliban wire wrap wound about his left testicle, down and around the split of his scrotum and thigh, up and wedged about the crack of his buttocks, lengthways to his abdomen, around his right shoulder, over to his left, and down again across his hairless chest. All this had been quickly and gracefully improvised and encircled about his body in the wee hours by his closest friends, these his comrades in arms. Habib couldn't cross his arms to relax his sternum to belch or lift his leg to fart. He was that uncomfortable.

In a pinch such as this, he as often thought longingly of the civil, caring, and absorbedly quiet conversations he and girlfriend Myrna had always had even when they first met. He at the two-top where he sat alone and observed. She, the wondrous, power-driven dervish, pranced and flailed at the edge of the stripper club's proscenium as only she could and knew how. He'd tipped in crisp, brand-new twenties each time the two had made eye contact. For two weeks running, she'd let him place the bills under her lacy, mid-thigh garter just because he looked like a *nice guy* and maybe a guy, a real rarity, that she could at long last trust. His smile seemed sincere, lusty for sure, but not too licentious, and certainly not like the others with their catcalls and whistles and their *take it all off* clarions. You might think a girl in her profession would get used to the seedy-sell vernacular, but she hadn't. So, Habib, he seemed a nice change of pace for a stage girl like her, a dancer no less hanging crotch-side up from a two-inch slender, erotic x fireman's pole in the middle of a room full of drunkenly deranged and horny voyeurs. That first night, she'd come off the stage covering herself with a backstage shawl and sat close enough to Habib just to see if her instincts were even palely attuned to being vaguely correct.

Like a gentle breeze in warm, filtered sunlight on the first day of spring was the way Habib remembered it. Myrna, her face, her voice, she was an understated trickle of clear creek water flowing past the mossy bend into a green straightaway and beyond toward the next unknowable oasis. Their connection was special for sure.

From Jehovah's Witness to his own personal quasi-converted Islamite, she would have agreed to just about anything (she'd plainly stated) if he'd pay her share of the next month's rent. So, she'd moved in … teddys, negligees, panties, jeans and blouses, eighteen pairs of shoes, four top coats, a hamper filled with sweaters, two lamps, and her rehearsal (stripper) pole … to his first floor, basement flat later on the same day, what's more within the same half hour. Besides, it was a Tuesday, and Tuesday was her night off which made it most convenient and doubly more affordable since her apartment rent was three months and five days in arrears.

No burkas (her words), or, she'd move out. Her position was stipulated up front and unmistakably so. Not in the cards (her words again), but for all intents and purposes, (he'd boasted aloud one day in an open room full of complete strangers) she was the *best fuck* of his (sexually inexperienced) life.

Okay, okay, confessed the apologetic Hobby, Habib Alif Ali-Ali. So, it was a Friday, a manly-man's, offhanded comment over backgammon by table three at the back of the hookah speakeasy just off South Bennington … and after work. Bravado, no less. Braggadocio, for sure. A flagrant yet flippant slip of the tongue. He admitted as much to her, Myrna, after she found out what he'd said. So, what if she was only the second woman with whom he'd had (sexual) relations? It's easiest to make up for these things (one's shortcomings ... one's perceived sexual inadequacies) in loose and ephemeral conversation (boastful, big talk no less) to perfect strangers he'd argued. Collective heedlessness, he'd called it or thought it, explaining it away as quickly and faultlessly as he could. They didn't know her; she didn't know them; no harm, no foul. He'd said all of that backing away from her out the front door and down the back stairwell, into his awaiting cab, his day job, calling back, 'But none of them have ever even been to the club to see you dance!'

'Like it mattered!' That's what she yelled back from down the hall just before she slammed the door, then ran to the other side of the room, and screamed out a window she'd frantically struggled to raise, 'Bastard!'

The other woman, the first woman, she was from Cairo. A prostitute, she claimed, a streetwalker by trade, of medium build with a youthful face and a soft, sandy complexion. She and he, the two of them together, they had skipped down a faintly lit back alley like school children and carried on atop a stubbly mattress of faded blue gingham draped over lumpy, cotton plait without bed linens, inhibition or regret. They could have been familiar partners or casually intimate friends the way they'd thrashed about ... almost as if they meant it or felt it ... a subliminal yet sultry connection, and most certainly past cordial ... or saw themselves as linked lovers amiss and perhaps making up for lost time. He remembered her that way even though it wasn't that way.

Even at the exchange of the carefully and correctly counted *geneh masri* (she'd held out her open hand politely with her palm upright, saying in a more business-like tone that she couldn't make change), the two then had smiled at one another with decency and at the same peculiar time made pleasant eye contact as they had shared almost everything else in the aforementioned brush.

As well, she had kissed his cheek like next of kin and called to him affectionately (he still believed this), out loud and quite audibly to say goodbye, telling him that he was her *Billy goat gruff*, in English no less, as she turned away though he didn't know the phrase much less the translation or the story's tale. Still, the memory remained wrapped in a provincial sweetness and sentimentality and was *their little secret* until this time.

Habib deliberated alone. Two pre-boarding passengers were in view. He sat sorrowfully and sulked and thought ...

If all goes according to plan, I will kill fifty to sixty people. Maybe one hundred. That is my highest estimate and best guess. More than likely, I will blow myself to smithereens and spew cartilage, epidermis, entrails, bone fragments and brain matter from here to there and likely do little more than rain human leftovers on a bunch of unassuming bystanders headed back to their workaday world ... bystanders attempting to make another loan payment or car installment or credit card advance. Best-case scenario, I have blown up a Celtics-Knickerbockers series season ticket holder of which I know nothing and care even less.

And yet, somehow, I am all in.

What the fuck am I doing? he heard himself ask.

As quickly and by mere coincidence, the Orange Line commuter train stopped in front of him, and he boarded in a cross-flank waddle. Southbound said the MBTA sign just outside the passenger window, then, off a graduated roll, he was swept forward and gone.

At the Ruggles Street subway exit island platform, on an anonymous, hot tip, Habib was picked up by seven, armed city policemen in safety goggles, headgear, and matching flak jackets with a small federal bomb squad standing by as backup on the next track over.

He did not object. He did not sigh. He did not whimper or protest or resist. He offered his wrists to be handcuffed and walked away amiably so that he could be loaded into an awaiting Pinkertons' wagon. He sat comfortably, silently shackled on the ride over to the downtown municipal jail. He voluntarily disrobed and unwired and de-detonated himself before entering the city's facility. It was all such a relief.

He was held in solitary (quarantined) and prosecuted with a court-appointed defense attorney by his side ... the one with thinning gray hair and thick, unbranded wire rims ... the same lawyer who had vainly attempted a shoddy or less-than-sensational plea bargain ... yet the crusty, old hoary judge, she would have none of it. There was just 'something suspicious about the whole thing,' the graceless yet rightful tartar scolded as she ordered up a sentence in months not days, years instead of months to cover her tracks or any traces of leniency should 'this thing' somehow come back to bite her.

But Habib had heard none of what the woman had said. Her words were a blur and a bad dream rolled into one. Through a long Plexiglass enclosure, from twenty feet away, Habib stiffly blew a goodbye kiss to his girlfriend (Myrna). He then shackle-shimmied down the exit ramp where he was loaded into a cosmopolitan blue prison van and whisked away inside a click, snap, and a wave.

Seven hours and twenty-two minutes later, he was officially inmate C-320962 and three doors down from a Blackfeet tribesman named Hiram Johnny Walker Quicksilver (the Indian resting on the bottom bunk of his own cell) and next door to a Mexican bandito named Jesús Ángel Escobar.

"¡Hola! ¿cómo estás?" The Mexican then yipped three times as a kind of staged hospitality and yelled out (more like a sarcastic and malevolent cat call), "Bienvenido a mi prisión, mi amigo!" (Welcome to my prison, my friend), his face-as-caricature pressed the entire time between two steel bars, while three guards and a fourth man escorted   Habib to his new zareba.

"And, welcome as well from me, too," said the warden hospitably holding open the cell door. "We've heard so much about you."

CHAPTER 21

Payback Under the Elm

Venganza Bajo El Olmo
Doris & Ned

*B*efore I was to go to the big city to meet the boss, City Chief, Escobar says he has called to tell me this little story. He called it a bedtime story, Escobar's cuento. I only answered the phone because I thought he wanted to tell me something about the upcoming job. But, no, it was just another one of his tales about Jesus the badass, reconquista Jesus. I should have known. Don't know why this one, but he started in before I could stop him. I guess he had to get it off his chest. I always listened to Jesus, but, sometimes, I just shook my head while I was listening, thinking, 'bro, what you gone and done now?'

Anyway, here goes. This is what Jesus said to me ... pretty much word for word.

Doris lived in a silver, double wide trailer with Ned. Ned was laid off, but Ned was always laid off. He parked his Harley under the elm tree in front of the house. The elm tree was the size of a small Ferris wheel. That's what Doris told Jesus so he could find the place. Jesus never said who he was. Doris parked her blue, not-so-new minivan

- 102 -

on the other side of the Harley closer to the tree trunk where less of the sun's rays fell. Tree pollen was always on the dash, but the shade left the car cool to entry when she got in and started it in the early a.m. to go to work at the chemical plant. She let Ned sleep in. Biker boy needed his beauty rest. That's what Jesus said Doris told him on the phone, biker boy needed his beauty rest.

Doris knew that Ned had been a hellcat in his day. He reminded her of it regularly. She waited on him while he was in prison. Once, she watched him hold his loaded Remington double barrel to the side of her head just for fun. Doris was in a headlock. ("Some fun, huh, Ned? Gran diversión, amigo." That's what Jesus says to me over the phone.) Doris, she coaxed Ned this way and that and talked him down from his Tapatio trip with a bold round of sweet talk, the whole time she's pushing her cleavage into his face as a distraction. You know, Jesus says, sex sells, el sexo vende. Ten or fifteen minutes go by. Maybe more. Doris is pleading. Ned, baby this, and Ned, baby that, she says, until Ned finally sees the light and lets her up and lowers the gun. Or, maybe, he was so cross-eyed drunk, he just couldn't find the trigger so he gave up and lowered the gun. Don't know, and as Doris said, "You never know. It's Ned."

Ned boasted about it more than once. As a matter of fact, Ned boasted about it every time someone stopped long enough to listen. The biker gangs, the twisted orgies, the drug hoe-downs, the all day, all night week-long binges that Ned claimed went on and on and on until every last one of them passed out or cratered in some lonely bar ditch twenty, thirty, forty miles from where the thing began. And, Doris would go along for the ride so to speak.

Tequila was Ned's drink of choice. He let you know that, too. "Them Mexicans are at least good for something," Ned would say. He followed that with some South American cocaína, then some local, 'homegrown' ecstasy and a stogie or two of Doris' greenhouse stash. It really was one for all, and all for one. Ned's biker buddies were sparkly tattooed, beaded and bearded, monogrammed and draped in loose *fitting animal pelts toting tire irons with metal medallions dangling from their handlebars, love handles, beer bellies, and all. They were a bunch of modern day Davy Crocketts on wheels. Chrome wheels. Throw in the designer drugs, and, you guessed it, 'we was hell on wheels.' (Ned's line.) Ned just dared anybody to challenge them cause he'd bust 'em. That's what Ned said. No one ever seen Ned fight, just talk a big game.*

In prison, Ned had stabbed a Mexican with a shank. The Mexican lived. After that, the two exchanged fierce and hateful glances at every mess hall chow time until Ned was paroled. (It was about right here in the telling that I remembered Ned. Jesus keeps going.) That was the story Ned told, but never mentioned the Mexican by name. Said if he had to do it all over again he'd have made sure the greasy, little spic died then and there; a second or third stab with that same shank would've done the trick. Ned loved to talk prison shit; It was a badge of honor.

Ned, even with his pot belly, he had large hands with broad, rough, and exposed knuckles. They stayed dirty morning, noon, and night. Doris said she liked her man's hands grimy, brawny and bare knuckled and particularly strong under her buttocks when they were getting it on. In fuck cadence, she screamed obscenities at Ned who said that he liked his women foul mouthed with great big tits and an ass to match. Said razor wire around a woman's bicep drove him wild. Berserk is what he said. That's what Doris said Ned said. Thinking about it and saying it out loud in front of company made Ned horney. He said that, too. He'd stand back with his hands on his hips and bay at the moon like a fully fed coyote in heat. "Don't cry for me, Argentina." That's what Ned said every time he finished telling the part about his woman and the razor wire on her bicep. Everyone always replied, Ah, Ned, you crazy son of a bitch! Tell us how you really feel. So, of course, Ned would back away and put his hands back on his hips and bay again at the moon like a fully fed coyote in heat and belt out the Argentina refrain all over again.

Jesus said he went to Ned's house to look him up. Pay him a little visit. Found Doris's name and number in the book. There was the elm tree. It really was the size of a small Ferris wheel. And, there was Ned's Harley parked in the shade just like Doris said it would be. She'd left for work. The minivan was gone. If nothing else, Jesus always prided himself on being on time. Puntual en Español.

Two knocks and Ned answered the door in his droopy Jockey shorts and a bleached wife beater. His belly'd grown so much since prison days, Jesus said he hardly recognized him standing on the other side of the shiny screen door with the swirly aluminum casing.

"Hell, se veía como, ... he (meaning Ned) looked like a fucking, knockoff Matisse," said Jesus.

"A what?" I said.

"A fucking Matisse," said Jesus. "And, not a real one."

Jesus was by this time brushing up on his art. That's what he said. He'd looked at some pictures in a book and memorized a few names. I asked again, "Matisse, what are you talking about, amigo?"

Jesus said, "It's French for money."

So, I said "Oh. Okay," nodded and let it go.

Anyway. That's what Jesus said he thought when he swung the door outward to get a better look at Ned to make sure it really was him. Then, Jesus said, "Fue el. It was him."

"Ned, you've aged quite miserably, amigo, old buddy, old pal," said Jesus.

Jesus was being proper to throw off Ned. And, it worked.

"And, who the fuck are you?" asked Ned in return. Ned stepped back as Jesus stepped just inside the screen.

"You mean you don't recognize me, bro'?" asked Jesus.

"Well, Jesus, Joseph, and Mary," replied Ned. His face was caught between mock sincerity and pure doubt. "It can't be," said Ned. "Escobar? I thought they'd buried your worthless carcass years ago. Heard you'd been electrocuted or lethally injected or took it up the ass so many times until you died."

"You wish," said Jesus.

Jesus pulled a shank from his trousers and stuck Ned deep in the gut. Jesus pulled out the shank, stepped back, stepped forward again, and stuck the shank again deeper into Ned's gut. Ned backed up five paces and fell into the middle of his football recliner. The game was going, but Ned was bleeding all over himself, looking down, and not watching.

"Payback, amigo," said Jesus as he watched a disoriented Ned bleed and suffer. "May vultures, with their talons perched on your pecker, chew on your balls for all eternity, eres gordito gordo, you fat slob." Then, he turned and walked out.

The aluminum screen door slammed behind him and latched itself shut.

Venganza.

Doris found Ned in the recliner when she came home from work. His face was washed out and real pale. The t.v. was still going, but Ned was just sitting there poker faced and unattentive in his bloody, bleached wife beater. His briefs were blood soaked as well. The shank was still stuck in Ned's gut where Jesus left it, and Ned had long since stopped breathing.

With unleavened emotion, Doris stood over Ned's droll corpse, looked down at him a second time, and said, "Ned, you know you had it coming."

She walked outside and rolled Ned's Harley (his kickstand left undisturbed) from under the elm over to the sunny side yard. She, then, backed her minivan into Ned's spot, from one side of the big tree to the other side of the big tree where the shade was best. It was the side she'd always wanted. With her cell phone in hand, she dialed 911 and told dispatch to send someone in an ambulance to come and pickup her husband. Said, "He's hurt real bad." As she hung up, Doris said to herself, "Beats praying."

Wise old Blackfoot Indian proverb says: Life is not separate from death. It only looks that way.

CHAPTER 22

Jesus Calls Back

"Hola, this is Jesus calling. Jesús Ángel Escobar," said Jesus. "We talked the other day. I'm sure you remember our conversation, amigo. I am calling you back about the painting, the painting you claim to be yours. You know, the one that D'Artagnan and I have in our possession. The painting over which you tried to kill me. That alone says a lot about the value of the painting, no?"

"Get to the point," said the man on the other end. It was City Chief. Jesus recognized his voice.

In prison, Jesus sketched from left to right the way he wrote. The sketches were always the same. Nudes. Women with subtle breasts and slender pelvic curves. Women with coal black hair, pouty red lips, and hauntingly dark eyes. He used the pencil the only way he knew to color their skin darker, Latino, heavier in tone than the prison paper. His sketches made the rounds. Rounds for masturbation. Rounds for cell sex. Some made the prison guards want Mexican women but never men. You could hear the catcalls, lurid and somewhat incestuous in tone from down the hallway when a sketch first made its way past the first show of hands. They were like the pretty new girl in the classroom on the first day of school. The oohhs and aahhs but cruder and more cruel, deeper and more flagrant in their desire.

"Oh, this is the best one, Escobar!"

"Draw another one, dude. She is so fucking hot."

"It's better than fucking your little sister before they threw me in here!"

Then the satanic laugh from off the painted wall which grew to a fever pitch until the guard would take the sketch away all to himself.

Jesus, he knew the magic in his hand. It gave life to the lifeless.

Jesus continued.

"If you have cooled down since the last time we talked, I will tell you my demands of how you can recover the painting you so much want returned. Si," said Jesus. He paused to let the man reply.

"I see," said City Chief, the man on the other end. "So, you are calling to extort money from me, is that it?"

"Si," said Jesus. "That is it. Your painting, assuming it is your painting, it is in a safe place. It is cared for. No harm will come to the painting, and it will be returned to you as long as I get what I deserve."

"Again. Get to the point," said the man. "How much?"

"Well, amigo," said Jesus, "Remember, it cuts two ways on this side. Dos. La mitad para mí. Half for D'Artagnan. D'Artagnan, he has to eat, too, you know. Plus, he needs new shoes to go with the new suit he has picked out ... you know, after we collect the money for the painting. Entender?" Jesus pressed the phone closer to his ear. He needed to hear the man's reaction clearly when he said what he was about to say. "This painting, your painting and the one in the safe place, I see that it is 'priceless', so to speak. I have looked this up, senor. I will say that for five million dollars, D'Artagnan and I can return the painting with no questions asked. Tu comprendes? Entiendes?"

"Five million dollars," said City Chief. "You are crazy. Even if I had that kind of money I wouldn't pay it. Keep the painting."

"Okay," said Jesus. "Como quieras. Suit yourself, amigo."

Jesus hung up.

Twenty minutes later.

City Chief called back. Jesus answered.

"Did you consider mi demanda, amigo?" asked Jesus. "Maybe we can work out some kind of a deal. D'Artagnan, he is willing. D'Artagnan and me, we are both razonables hombres, amigo."

"For you two freeloaders, I tell you what I will do," said City Chief. "I will give you the design of my next project. It makes the others pale by comparison. If you and D'Artagnan step in and help, I will cut you in on the deal, but at the end of the deal you return the painting that you have stolen from me. It is up to you."

"I am always willing to listen to deals, amigo," said Jesus. "But, for the time being the painting that you claim as yours stays in the safe place as insurance. Ningul n daño, ninguna falta. (No harm, no foul.) This way I am safe and alive. Seguro de vida. I am sure you understand me since it was you that shot out D'Artagnan's mirror while aiming for me. Recuerdo, amigo? I am sure you remember this. I am still looking over my shoulder night and day."

CHAPTER 23

Aamsskaapipikani VII
Blackfeet Nation VII

It was a note. It read ...

We go to Isabella's garden, the museum. We take the pictures and otras obras (other works) off the wall. (May need pliers or a screwdriver. Don't know. I will have both in my pants (pantalones) pocket.) Then, we leave out the back door and go home. Vete a casa. Little to no traffic that time of night. Subway runs 24/7. In two, three months we party hardy, fiesta robusta, amigo. It was signed Jesus.

There are two night guards at Isabella's garden. Fred and Barney. This is what the boss man says. Jesus and me (cellmate one two eight four eight two and cellmate one two eight four eight three, me and him.), we call them Fred and Barney, you know, Flintstone and Rubble. Boss, he says take them out first. Gag them after you cuff them. Put paper sacks over their heads or blindfold them, something so they can't see. Put them in the broom closet down the hall on the first floor (points to it on the map with his index finger) or downstairs in the women's bathroom (a stall each) for safekeeping. Both are big enough for two people. He points this out, too, on the map. The one is here (the broom closet); the other one is down the steps and over there. We are all in. A couple of tokens, he called the two men. Two patsies, stoolies but in the way. Hourly wagers, the official uniforms in cop blue, the name tags above the badges, the lopsided cap with insignias and a badge as shiny as a baby's butt over the mop of hair, too long for a real cop, says Boss City. I got it. Jesus gets it, too. Some squiggly painted pictures on a chalkboard is nothing to die for, says Boss, no matter how old or valuable or how much money somebody says they're worth or what somebody else claims them to be. The two can't even steal stuff to make it worth their while, so they're just there and barely covering their monthly rent. Take it from an ex Marine and tribal warrior. All that fighting, and still, I got nothing.

The two men, they drink black coffee with sugar by the tablespoon to try and stay awake until shift's done. It never works, says Boss. Then, he says, the place is ours.

I know what he means.

Jesus, he knows what Boss means. We both nod.

The place is ripe for the picking.

You only live once, kemosahbee.
One pass. Chute opens. Ride 'em cowboy.
(Bumper sticker on my old, worse for wear horse trailer.)

In death, I want a pyre the length of a full semi-tractor trailer. Maybe two. Or say, the span of twenty stallions lined head to tail in single file. Same height or higher. A load of dried spruce underneath, maybe some sagebrush and oak wood, too. Pine burns nice and with a sweet smell. That would do. The scent will drift for miles. I will smell like smoky perfume heavenward in the burn. People for miles in every direction will stop what they are doing to sniff the air and get a whiff of my charred Indian ass going up in flames for the last time. There he goes, they will say. Hiram Johnny Walker Quicksilver, the Indian's Indian. Rodeo rider, warrior brave, lover, and fighter. Didn't take shit from no one. Now he is gone. Bless the man (they will say) that don't take shit from no one and bless you Hiram Johnny Walker Quicksilver. They *will say all of this. The flames billowing up to the open cloudlessness will touch the tip of the stars in the big sky, and then I can finally meet up with this God dude, the Great Spirit of the Blackfoot Confederacy ... the One that never answers in my private calls, my conversations in confidence, my cries for help, or the secret messages and codes that I have sent out along the way over all this time.*

(Perusing the setting, reining in his thoughts, Hiram continued.)

Sure. I can see it now. Death is never so far away or so forgotten that I cannot see it or cannot imagine what it must look like.

You can see me. I am here in front of you now in plain view.

So, look into my eyes.

You can see that I am not afraid to die.

I, the Piegan-Blackfeet brave and Algonquian warrior, even in this modern, merciless and unforgiving world, will ask the Great Heavenly Chief in the big sky, the one with the full, crested eagle feather war bonnet adorning His swelled head ... I will ask Him this, in this way, and in a loud voice:

"Hey, God. You! Hey, why you never answer any of my messages?"

That is what I will say to him because I am not afraid.

Too, I will say,

"Dude, if You gave two shits, or if You had any manners, You would have said, Hey, Hiram Johnny Walker Quicksilver, I am too busy. Bigger fish to fry. Will get back with you later, little brother."

That's all You needed to say, oh mighty Emperor Itákkaa, King Kemosahbee. How hard could it be? Was this too much to ask?

(Hiram Johnny stepped back. He drew another breath deep into his broad chest. He shook his head, a head shake between weary disbelief and tolerant disgust, then he began again.)

But, in the end, in this the final sundown, I am betting that God, the grand caretaker, He is not there. He has checked out. Or, He wasn't never there in the first place. And, that in the end, it is just my ashes in a tiny, little heap somewhere among the ash pile of oak and blue spruce, pine and sage lying there when all is said and done. You cannot tell any of these things apart after the first snowfall much less after the spring rain begins to wash away the dirty ice patches up against the clean river bank. You know this. My ashes and the oak and the pine and the blue spruce, they are then little more than runoff to the open meadow below where the elk and the buffalo graze, summer into next winter's spring.

But, like I have said, you know all of this so you know what I mean.

My squaw, Esther, she can pretend though. And, she can then sprinkle the gray dust into the dark water of the beaver pond up above the coyote den or tip my remains into and along the water's edge of the clear, still trout stream. It won't matter none. I am dead. The pure water will wash away all of me in the blink of a stout and strong and bull-necked night owl. I am then little more than a memory in the minds of the people that I have touched for better or for worse.

(But, for you to know, while I am alive and talking big, I admit that I like the idea of the trout stream, the gentle trickle of the big creek best. Me and my leftovers settled amongst fresh water as clear as the moon's glow in winter cold. This makes me smile.)

Ashes to ashes. That is what people tell me. Then, so be it.

Anyway.

I hear people say that they want to die in their sleep. Peaceful like. You know. No pain. They are covered up in their blankets and dressed in their woolen nightgowns and furry caps and darned socks and out of nowhere death sneaks up on them at the foot of their bed and snuffs out the candle. All breathing stops. The dream ends. There is a final last gasp, a heave, maybe even a sigh to finish things off, but you are now dead. Welcome to The Black Hole ... so to speak. More than likely it is akin to your last night's stay in the back room in some abandoned, mountain guest lodge beside the noisy ice maker that is now broken, or a mistaken stopover at some stale, cheap-ass motel where the cars park up close and in front of the over-painted (green to red to purple then back to green) front door that opens into your cheap-ass room. I guess it is so. Don't know for sure. Haven't been there yet. You fall face first into the unshaken abyss like it is a stagnant water trough where nothing happens from there because you can't remember shit and nobody comes back to tell what it was like.

But this is not for me.

I have thought about this many times for what it is worth. (Like you have a say in how you die.) So, I will stake my claim and say it here in front of all the world.

For me, Hiram Johnny Walker Quicksilver, tell them each and every one that I want to die in a hail of gunfire. Lead is flying. Shrapnel, too. People, brave people and cowards alike all around are ducking for cover and covering their asses with whatever and however they can. Bullets are everywhere like raindrops in a heavy thunderstorm.

But, not me, the warrior. I stand tall under the siege staring at the masked devil of death because I owe him nothing and he expects me to cower and retreat. So, I cry out, "Surprise, devil imitáá (dog). I am a son of a son of the bravest Blackfeet, Bull Bear ... a cousin, too, of the wise and great chief Sitting Bull. For me, Hiram Johnny Walker Quicksilver, it is Little Big Horn all over again and in the flesh. It is me and Custer (the devil himself). We are face to face, saber to tomahawk, lance to spear. And, I am not afraid.

It is boot camp, too, but worse. The air is full of smoke, USMC smoke and grenade explosions and mortar shells and rockets scorching the night air. Shattered debris is all around, everywhere in the milky dusk. The stench of hundreds of downed men has once again desecrated the natives' land. I am little more than the slaughtered bison or the encircled coyote and the slain deer and elk and the mountain lion that is no longer even home to his own mountain.

Funny how in my dreams, I have hated the white man, but in the waking, we get along pretty good. They are all not so bad anymore I guess.

If not that, then I will stand in the open plain, war bonnet, face paint, spear and shield facing and watching as the oncoming stampede of a thousand or more bison approaches. Their hooves are thunder.

They appear like a fur coated cavalry of bandits and marauders, all headed for me.

Look out, some would say. Hiram Johnny Walker Quicksilver, you are about to be trampled to death.

You must run for your life, they cry out.

But, no, I stand fast. Tall, then taller still. I am a brave. A warrior by trade. A warrior by birth. Áwaawahkao'tsii. This will never change, not even in death's charge even when with purpose it is all around me and moving toward me at breakneck speed. The bison, they will split in pairs when they see the Blackfeet man standing all alone because they respect the man that is not afraid to die. For certain, that is me. If not, it is my time to go. Tell this to the world, but Esther, she knows this already. No need to grieve. No need for the silly white man's prayers. Our god and reason for being are different even if we are both somehow men sharing common ground.

Iiyikitapiiyit! Be fearless.

And you, too, must be brave and fearless in death because it will come for you whether you like it or not, whether the time is right for you or wrong.

I know what you are thinking. I have heard the same voice many times. More Indian claptrap and sour grapes from another tough luck Indian, these voices say. Oh, poor red man, I feel so sorry for you. (This same voice says so in his mocking tone.) You Indians cry so long and hard over spilled milk. Hey, says the unrepentant white man, your papoose never had it so good. You got your reservation land. You got your tribal laws and council. You got your cash casinos to go with your moccasins and turquoise. You now take back what you say you lost and then some. What more could you want, you filthy rich fuck?

But the Indian at the top learned from the white man at the top. Keep what you got to yourself. Comes from being at the top. Screw the little man, the little pigtailed, braided Indian on the bottom of the totem pole. Let him keep his turquoise and paint horse, his wigwam and his toothless, fat squaw. You've got the money.

Yeah, so what if the white man let us have a few of his casinos so that we could become fatter and lazier and less motivated to work than before. From stouthearted warrior brave to pudgy blackjack dealer ... there is something wrong and blurry with this picture.

My death will be with bow and arrow and tomahawk in hand. But so that I can fell more white devils at one time, I will use his automatic weapons and cut their heads off with a twist at the waist, my finger glued to the trigger.

Hiram's squaw, she can then sell the art painting for big money to another thief or to someone that can look the other way. Get a young buck, saahkinaawa, with a hard-on twenty-four seven and live happily ever after. She will be worth millions of Abraham Lincolns and millions and millions, too, of George Washingtons. I can see her laughing now her belly jiggling, tits too, with all that money covering her and the top of our mattress.

She'll bathe in it. Count it every evening before bed. Between 'Price' and 'Wheel' (of Fortune), she will say this. For her, that is saying something for sure. Her money will never see a bank ... the white man's vault for white man's currency. Nothing Indian about the men on the paper. No Geronimo. No Sitting Bull. No Tonto. No Lone Ranger either. Just a lot of old timey white men with wooden teeth and bushy unscalped heads ... hair like Quonset barrack mops turned upright in their buckets one and all.

Okay, okay, for sure. Enough for now. Big talk only gets you so far in this life. Little more than dog's barking in the distance. Tomorrow, aapinákos, it is another day. We will see which paths cross and where they lead.

Hiram Johnny Walker Quicksilver laughed out loud.

He enjoyed himself sska' (extremely) in the moment.

He had listened to himself speak and liked what he had heard.

CHAPTER 24

Witten Kingsland?

Third floor. Suite 311. Sirin Enterprises. Imani Kahn, orthonym Witten Kingsland … that is who he was. As the owner and sole proprietor, he held the cordless telephone receiver comfortably up against his left ear and pressed answer, but as quickly, it seemed that he had been put on hold. He sat still in a leather lounger with an open bag of *Rudy's* friendly fried pork rinds in his lap and munched away while listening for a response on the other end and slicing a red apple into quarters and pausing to brush away the crumbs from his tweed woolen trousers. He took a full swig of his German beer from the green bottle, swallowed, nervously picked and peeled at the pilsner label, and spoke up indiscriminately clearing his throat. "Uh hmm."

"Witten Kingsland, sir, got a guy here on the other line that says he knows you." This man was a secretary or retainer-flunky, answering service of sorts.

"Okay. Could you get his name?" And, again he was on hold.

Kingsland, last name. First name Witten. An immigrant and a Jew, and a *self-loathing* Jew what's more. He'd heard the phrase once years before, the *self-loathing* bit, duly researched and defined it as one's own self-hatred and denigration and dislike, and so clung to the notion because it made it easier to cope with his disguise and deceit, the thievery and his amorality. It captured his outward persona and how he wanted himself to be portrayed. *Self-loathing*, it had a snappy and self-serving ring to it all its own and covered tracks that as of yet hadn't been laid down or hollowed out, much less devised and put into motion.

Anguished, too, (another catchall that he loved) ... it made for a guiltlessly comforting façade, and, as conveniently, left *conscienceless* out of the mix entirely. He hid all of it so exceptionally well, and, at least as well as his loathsome intolerance of those others, the clueless masses, and the rest of nescient humankind. He was good at *lumping shit together* just for the sake of it, you know, time constraints and workaday intangibles like neatness and orderliness and fastidiousness.

Posing as an Arab, and a religious Arab at that ... how clever an idea! A selective stroke of genius. He measured himself by the mastery of his own manipulative magic, case in point, his own, personal inner circle of Middle Eastern henchmen who at the drop of a hat would do his bidding.

His Arab getup was hanging on a wooden hanger alongside his cashmere top coat and neck scarf next to the open window beside the antique dresser. Above that was a Giacometti, *Woman with Her Throat Cut*. Across and to the right a Klee, *Aged Phoenix* alongside *Sumpflegende (Swamp Legend)*. The next wall over where there had been a vacant space Braque's *A Girl with a Cross* beside a second Braque, his *Violin, Mozart and Kubelick*. On the small narrow wall, *Landscape with Cottages* hung subtlety-lit by a single-bulb, tarnished art lamp which up close allowed the viewer to see the artist's name Rembrandt van Rijn by way of an unencumbered, cursive flick of the master's own most nimble wrist.

Man With a Pipe hung crooked but stood out, pronounced simply by virtue of its cubist flair, images embedded in and amongst other images; after all, it was a Metzinger. *Mandolin and Guitar*, Picasso's own, sat on the floor in a lean up against a tall, colorful porcelain vase but as of now it had yet to be deservedly displayed elsewhere in some other more prominent station in this, his small, two-room city apartment. But, there were dozens of paintings and sculptures stacked sideways and at crossed angles like bric-a-brac in a flea market bin because there simply wasn't room. Many of the collectibles were merely lying about in a clutter or something of a heap, untagged and unnamed. Dishevelment sat atop card tables two, three, and four, its replica on the Medici credenza, and littered a second Georgian sideboard and the twin giltwood taborets stuffed in the unfrequented far corner of the apartment's second room.

Gain their attention (he'd say to himself) by whatever means (distract, distract, distract) and steal the artwork at random. Quietly. Coolly. Breathlessly if possible. The less fanfare the better, his watchword always. But most of all, *Reverently*, the same way they have been stored and housed because they are so impetuously and irrationally and garishly worshipped. *Reverent theft* to coin his phrase. The thought seemed polite enough as if it alone covered correctness from all its angles in some thief's stodgy, prim-and-proper etiquette enchiridion that he used as a playbook.

"Okay. Name's Habib," said the secretary-retainer picking up where he'd left off. "Habib Ali or Alif Ali. Something like that. Museum artwork. Collectibles. Missing pieces. Something. Can't read my own writing, but sounds like it's right up your alley, Mr. Kingsland."

"Yes. Got it. Put him through."

Kingsland paused to listen then spoke up, "Yes, Habib. So nice to hear your voice again."

CHAPTER 25

A'póóhsin Aakáítapissko
Trip to the Big City

When I left the trailer in the evergreens to go to the big city, I took Esther's sister's Cadillac. I promised her that I would bring it back in one piece, cleaned up, and with a full tank of gas. A good deal for Esther's sister because she was always broke. For me, it was a good deal because the big sedan got better highway mileage than my pickup. More comfortable, too, on the big, eight lane interstate. It was plush and roomy ... roomy enough for three saddles ... halters, bridles, and blankets to match. Plus, I knew that I would look more like a businessman, an Indian business man, so to speak, if I was driving the big sedan. I took the war bonnet silk screen and the steer busting logo out of the back window so I was not a dead giveaway for a misplaced Indian, ex con, rodeo rider, tribal warrior, tomahawk chopping mother fucker when I got to the big city. I know you can understand.

Esther's sister's husband, he was a steer roper and dogger like me. He rode some broncs back when we was younger. Turned out on a dozen or more brahma, as well. Esther's sister's husband, he loved rodeo almost as much as me. And honestly, he was a good hand; won some go-rounds and one or two trophies as I recall. A belt buckle, too. But, honestly, he was not as good as me.

We sometimes used the same horse to heel. We sometimes trailered our horses together when we went to the big events. A long way there and back and a lot of expense not counting entry fees. Sometimes we swapped ropes to see whose was the best, the best drape, the best feel and stiffness, good tension, and so forth for the best loop. And, I must admit, he won me over from three eighths to seven sixteenths. (Talking lariats here. Rodeo dialect.) I caught more steers after that. Calves, too. And quicker. I always give Esther's sister's husband a big shout out for that. No prize money, but a big shout out. I kept the prize money for tie rods. (Another Hiram one liner to keep you on your toes, and a good one. Tie rods, you have to admit that's a really good one.)

The Cadillac was nice. Esther's sister had special ordered the Indian blanket seat covers in blood scalp red (Quicksilver Indian joke, 'blood scalp red'. No offense, Custer.) and teepee turquoise. There was a big face of an Indian chief embroidered on the one side toward the shoulder of the fold. It made me feel like I was charging into battle with Sitting Bull atop his pinto, me just driving down the highway and riding on top of the weave. I admit I whooped real loud several times before I hit the interstate I was so excited. Then, once or twice more for good measure and good fortune fifty, sixty miles out. I always believed in the good vibes and the great spirit, a'pistotooski, and all that. Most of it, anyway. Good luck, too. (Bad luck, sometimes, as well.) No explaining nothing, but I know you understand.

CHAPTER 26

Shawnee Mae Meskwaki
&
The Vatican Loaner

Jesus, he told me this in the early morning. Me and him, we were in the same room at the cheap motel. It was kind of like old times, the two of us in the same confined space. Booked it under José and Maria Sanchez for twenty-five dollars a night. We paid cash for three nights. An extra night just in case. I told him he was Maria, I was José. So, don't go there, bro', is what I told him.

We had just pulled in. Set our bags aside and started to relax.

Jesus sat upright, pillows against the headboard, legs stretched out, socks, no shoes, dressed only in his prison briefs. Again, like old times. He smoked a cigarette with his right hand, a joint with his left. He blew smoke rings first and watched them spin away, then, with his left hand, he inhaled deep into the next breath like it was his last. There was fire all around. Like a medicine man inside a teepee, so I listened.

I had the motel straight back in a perfect lean up against the side wall with my cowboy boots on top of the motel telephone book (thicker than a beaver dam, ksisskstaki). I was comfortable enough so I could be curious and pay attention.

Jesus, he said to me, "City Chief has a girlfriend, novia. She is fine."

He looked my way.

"Really fine," he said. "Muy bien, amigo."

He smiled like only Jesus could. Satan had nothing on Jesus.

"Legs up to here," he said. He put his hand up and leveled out chest high.

"Tetas out to there," Jesus said. His right and left hand both moved out and away to the front of his chest at arm's length. "Meskwaki (fox), my indio valiente and Blackfoot warrior," said Jesus. Then, he smiled broad-like, like Jesus being Jesus, himself. "Zorro frío de piedra, amigo. One stone cold fox, and then some."

"What's more," he said almost admirably and proudly, "How do you say, *el lardón lardón*? She is the thief's thief."

That is what Jesus told me ... like they were kin.

I don't know. I never seen her, I said, and I never seen City Chief either. But, that is what Jesus said to me so I said, "Okay," so he would finish the story and I could go back to what I was doing. I imagine this woman, the Meskwaki, but that is as far as it goes.

Jesus said, "City Chief and his girlfriend, they see this announcement in the newspaper ... Vatican art on exhibit at local convent. It is like an invitation to Lucifer himself."

"So, this girlfriend, City Chief's girlfriend," Jesus tells me this, "She joins the nunnery." There is a twinkle in his eye.

"She arrived with a small satchel or bolsa. In it was a change of underwear, a clean pair of socks, a purple, tie-dyed t shirt, a bra, a hair brush, a sweatshirt that said I Love Jesus, and a small Bible. The Bible was hollowed out with a snap closure to carry her pink, *Hello Kitty* Glock. The pistol, it was fully loaded.

Roadside, she removed her two nose studs, her seven earrings from the right side, the five from the left, the six silver bracelets, and her gold embroidered cowboy boots, this just before she stepped out of the shiny black sedan into the evening breeze. It was the car that dropped her off at the road leading to the monastery chapel at the top of the hill. She'd signed on the day earlier, given her vows to a holy nun alongside a silent, stoically-faced, and reverend monk, and promised to return by dusk the following day. The next day, by all accounts, she was early. But, her purpose was only to steal art, religious art, art of whatever kind. It made no *diferencia*."

"The woman, mujer del diablo, she has no religion. Ninguna religión," said Jesus. "There is nothing in her soul, nothing in her bones that might resemble conscience. Sin conciencia," said Jesus. "She is more guiltless than me."

This from Jesus so I listened more closely.

"This woman," said Jesus, "the girlfriend, she is a real pro. Un verdadero profesional al máximo."

Jesus said that in the first hours of the first day, City Chief's girlfriend had found her man. She made eyes at this fellow, this monk. Brother Malcolm, hermano católico, was his name. He was wearing a cowl. She whispered to him from inside the chapel at their introduction. At first, she made eyes at him over breakfast. Then, she sat across from him at lunch. She smiled. She batted her eyes. The third time, she looked around, looked back to the man, this monk, and winked. She wet her lips. She flicked her tongue and wet her lips again. This man, Malcolm, he was paralyzed.

Next, she followed him to the evening meal. Where he went, she was close behind. She was quick with a *seductora* and licentious smile and made herself like an offering from on high from God Himself. This man, Brother Malcolm, he was a monk, what's more a Trappist monk. He was also, more or less, the turnkey to the abbey's art room as vault. He kept the band of keys tied to his naked waist beneath the sash that gathered and completed his cassock. The six keys draped about his belly and batting junto a sus testículos (up against his testicles), it was the closest to sex this man had ever come.

The Resurrection of Jesus. It was en prestamo del Vaticano (on loan from the Vatican). It was the reason the meskwaki, this Shawnee

Mae woman had arrived. City Chief's girlfriend, she knew this. Ella lo sabio, amigo, con certeza. City Chief knew this, too.

She began to whisper into Brother Malcolm's ear, "Shawnee Mae, Shawnee might, Shawnee Mae, Shawnee might," over and over and over when no one was looking. "Shawnee Mae, Shawnee might," she said again and again pressing her chest, her splendid cleavage into his cheek, this as well when no one is looking. She said things to this man that he had never heard. Dirty things. Palabras sucias. Sexual things. In detail and graphic adorno. Things that are difficult for other people, close to one another, to say or hear or listen to. And yet she said these things to a man who knows not his manhood, amigo. A religious eunuch. A man in name only. A man who is ashamed of his erection, his stamina, his station in the natural order of being.

She teased and titillated this poor, speechless man in every way imaginable until the hour she whispered to him, "Meet me in the cloak room across from the antechamber, Brother Malcolm. I have something to show you." She then moved closer, like the spider to the fly, to silently silhouette the one word, "Me." This to a man that knew only that his penis, pene, was for splattering urine into a porcelain vessel or breaking the pitch of the metered to and fro, back and forth of the antechamber and art room keys, the ones that he kept dangling under his robe. This was such a surprise!

And, of course, he solemnly agreed. What, did you think he would refuse?

"The God, dios, el Gran Hombre en el cielo," said Jesus, "Maybe He has his place, amigo, but so does the beautiful woman, mujer muy, muy, muy hermosa, says one man to another."

They met in the cloak room at midday. He was quite nervous. He knew, too, however, that he was very aroused though aroused he'd never been so it was confounding to him in the throw. Meskwaki was ready and waited for him like a hunter in a blind. When he entered, she was already there waiting, erect like a risen and disrobed Pietá, looking proudly submissive, a holy yet wanton temptress, God's lamb only begotten as one. Disrobed, she stood ever-present before the stolid monk like his own Mary Magdalene, scripture come alive. Malcolm, he was lonely and even more easily smitten in the moment.

They fell to the floor like two unfed predators over a fresh carcass. Sister Shawnee whispered sultry, filthy, inflected and instructive language to the man, this man who had never known pleasure. He was putty in her hands. In the unframed moment, she taught him all that she knew. Their muted sounds soon resonated outside the stone walls. Brother Malcolm could be heard writhing and flailing and calling on the one Jesus, God the father and the Holy Ghost, the virgin Mary, both Saint Peter and Saint Paul. City Chief's girlfriend (Sister Shawnee Mae by then) coddled and caressed and suckled and fornicated with him for some time until his time expired. For Malcolm, it was eternity calling. He had never had it so good.

But, Brother Malcolm, he had no chance. The dude, this man, he'd finally found his God and his son Jesus for sure, and all this in spite of his religion." Jesus paused. He smiled broadly, and as quickly, relished his most sinister chuckle as only Jesus Angel Escobar could. "But it was not for long, amigo. No, no, no. Sister Shawnee Mae Shawnee Might, she took Malcolm's keys from his robe pocket, drew her pistola from her Biblia, shot him once in the face and in a flash turned the gun on the other nun who had just walked in and caught them in the cloak room together. This same rogue Sister, meskwaki Shawnee Mae, she then stood over the dead monk and said, "How dare you molest one of your own, you pervertido."

"El ladrón ladrón," said Jesus. "Entiendes ahora, amigo? Si? Get it? See, what I tell you. Las bolas de un hombre. There can be no doubt, amigo, the balls of a man."

Sister Shawnee Mae, as she left the convent chapel, miss meskwaki took her favorite painting, *The Resurrection of Jesus,* el Rembrandt and the loaner from the Vaticano, from the vault.

She grabbed all the other pieces that she could carry, the ones she wanted, from the vestibule, pitched the dead brother's keys into the shrubbery, and skipped out the back. Pulled it off clean as a whistle.

The thief's thief, like I said.

The black car, el sedán, was waiting at the bottom of the hill in the same place where Meskwaki had been dropped off just days before.

When the young woman, City's meskwaki, walked into The Quick Locker, her habit had fallen sideways past her left shoulder, the look of a broached sombrero from a hard and fast ride into a stiff headwind. She'd pulled her sequined cowboy boots over her nun socks and tucked the length of her scapular downward and crossways into her tight-fitting jeans. It looked more like a bad costume than what it really was ... a religious imposter gone bad and in a quick change.

On aisle J, she took the pieces, one by one, out of the croker sack and placed them carefully into locker number 59. It was row J. She could hear the attendant talking to her from behind the glass across the way. She deflected his instruction in a turn. She flipped the lock back into place, stuck the key into her pocket, and walked past the cashier's window without a passing glance. In another minute, she walked down the open street and slipped into the front seat of a black sedan. In an instant, she was gone.

Jesus said to me, "I found the key, la clave."

Taking a final, deep draw from his marihuana cigarrillo, he said, "The key to Locker 59. You know, the one in the dead man's (D'Artagnan) pocket. The key and the lock. La pintura, The Resurrection of Jesús, remember, with the character that is the same name as me, it was in the trunk all nice and neat. But, you know that already, Quick. When all is said and done, the key, it is yours, amigo. I will have enough (recompensa) for one man when we are finished here."

Jesus exhaled hard like a swimmer coming up for air and then smiled mordantly behind the thick cloud of white smoke.

"You see I am like this imposter nun, this Sister Meskwaki, Shawnee Mae. We will all go to our grave with our own *rights* ... you know, those things in this life that we have done right and correctamente ... our own *wrongs*, too ... as will I ... you know, those things that we have done not so well, incorrecto, or with mala intención.

So then, tell it to your God. Show Him how *right* you were when you are dead. Or, show Him how *wrong* you were for all the right reasons. It is all the same.

As for me, I will die in vain and live with the consequence of my life in the hereafter but only if there is one."

Jesus leaned back when he had finished. In this, his motel moment of enlightenment, he felt satisfied like a hallowed mahatma. As quickly, he grinned and then laughed excitedly, crazy-like, as if it were all just a show and some kind of flippant reassurance to himself over his own brand of quantified madness. But looking again, his dialogue was little more than a jaded respite of word-splash toward his next long draw, an even deeper drag of fresh white smoke from his marihuana conjunta.

CHAPTER 27

Nipápao'kaanistsi
In My Dreams

In the talking dream, ipapaino, this is what I see.

It is me again. I am in the here and now. The vision is clear and real and more lifelike than life itself. The colors are brighter in the dream than those in broad daylight or the clear cast of a prism in summer sun, summer rain. Too, I can even reach out and touch the silver buckle that cinches tight my leather chaps just below the curved line of my young belly. Hiram Johnny Walker Quicksilver, my initials are stenciled down the length of the dark leather leg, the purple fringe offsetting the black drape and sanguine piping and cross-stitched tomahawks. These chaps, they are by my design. That is what the dream tells me. Of my many prison dreams, this is the one I most remember.

Maybe somehow this dream, it will help you to know me, the Blackfoot warrior, better. Then again, maybe not. I can never tell how a dream or a story or a splinter of hearsay will sway people to this side or that, pro or con. Maybe it just confuses them in the throw. Or, maybe it simply poisons the circumstance and prevents the two from knowing one another the way that they might were the truth laid bare. You never know. It is another one of life's mysteries. Something else to deal with for certain.

Maybe you will get to know the art thief, too. Maybe. Maybe not. Tough to say.

Not the same, but sort of.

We do what we do, then our time, a'paisii, it runs out. Like it or not.

Hiram, he points to himself and the middle of his broad and thick chest.

In my dream, me and Habib, we are there together. Somehow. Some way. Strange, you ask? Yes, it is strange. It is for you to know that this is way back in time. The two of us in this dream, you could say, for better or for worse. I do not know why. It just is. No explaining.

(Hiram pauses, draws a deep breath, then continues.)

This is what the dream tells me, and that is all that I know.

He points behind and over his shoulder. Way back. He keeps pointing and smiling. Further still. For emphasis, Hiram says this once more. He points again with his thumb extended over his shoulder a second time to indicate _ *'go back in time even further'* ... a hitchhiking gesture yet higher ... an umpire's call (a close call) at home plate. Whatever. He shakes his head a second time. He waves his hand as if he were shooing a lone fly to sweep away the image.

Let me begin so that you can follow my story.

This dream began by itself although, as I have said, it is a time that has passed, a time when my pants fit looser... my belt tighter ... but like I say, it is still me, and I am in Belle Fourche. This much I remember. Belle Fourche fairgrounds, and the arena, and chute number three. I know chute number three because I remember it for what it was. The hinge is broken on the left side toward the top of the gate. One bull too many, but it is easy to say that now. Big weld holding it in place. Good enough for government work, I always say, and good enough for the annual summer rodeo. Good enough, too, for kids hanging on it in the yearlong off-season fantasizing and calling out the names of their famous cowboy heroes like they were them. So, chute number three, it will have to do because this is what the dreams tells me.

Belle Fourche is a big arena for sure, but in the dream, the arena is even bigger than the one I remember from my full-time employment as a rodeo rider back in my cowboy days.

Many, many people have filled the stands (too many to count it seems) and magically, there are now even more people than the rodeo arena can hold. In a clear vision, these people, they are hanging from unsturdy lamp posts while others are dangling from the sag of colorful cloth bunting. The loyal and faithful followers, the true, tireless diehards, are draped from splintered rafters and perched like buzzards upon stadium girders and leaning out long ways over untrustworthy railings, suspended idly, and stacked in a sprawl from support timbers in single file, all this just to get a better view. Girlfriends are astraddle their boyfriends, shoulder high. Babies, too, upright, their little backs straight like curious prairie dogs from a lookout hole, and very attentive for they must know early on that they will be the next generation to bear the rodeo cross like a sacred religion all its own. There are newborns held even higher, two-handed, still and motionless up into the air so they can see what they should see. Girls and boys stare hard through the cracks of raddled bleachers and scramble to peek through the crevices of old men's bowed legs, in and around and through the open pleats of women's skirts and younger cowgirls' even fancier frills. They are all there looking and waiting and anticipating the next cowboy, the next bull rider, in order that they might measure him as a man, as a rodeo performer, as the cowboy he pretends and works and wants to be. That cowboy, it is me ... Hiram Johnny Walker Quicksilver.

This is a very big moment indeed, and one for all the world to see. My dream tells me these things in colors and shapes and sounds and scenery all of which I recognize. And, look, there I am. I see myself, somehow, moving to the top of the railing and finally taking my seat atop the moment for this is my hope's hope and my dream's dream. It is both says the talking dream speaking to me in fluent Siksiká no less.

But, do not worry, kemosahbee. I am ready, and I am next up. "Chute number three," like I said because I can then hear the public-address announcer call my name, "Hiram Johnny Walker Quicksilver," over the loudspeaker at this very moment. It is a clear voice, one from heaven. God-Rodeo is speaking. Hokahey. Hokahey!

"Sái'piyit," cries the Indian rider.

"Charge!" cries a cheering rodeo Custer from outside the chute wishing me well.

These people filling the stands are people that know me and that I know, that cheer me, that revere me ... me, the rodeo cowboy, the Indian brave as bull rider, that revere their rodeo, the game and the sport as one, like it was their great grandfather's dated photograph to be looked upon with genuine warmth and even greater respect. It is a time and place that came before you so you must do good ... you must do better even than what you think you must.

These same people, they pay their hard-earned money, and so it is that they will pay even closer attention. They know every cowboy, all of them, present and past because history here matters. They know and savour, too, the mix of performers, athletes say some, one and all. And, it is for their talents and hard work, their accomplishments and trials, the athlete, the performer, both man and beast, these people have come here to watch.

And, even though it is a dream, I, too, know this place very well.

When I look out, I recognize the weathered faces, and I know most of their names as well. I know the chiseled landscape, too. I know every twisted corral, its every dingy chute, its every cross tied runway, its every pocket, puddle, and footpath, dog track and horse trail, each of them within a stone's throw and shouting distance of the greensward from where I stand to gaze. I know the smells of its broken earth, its busted sod, and the scent of the worn saddle leather and the sacred stench of sweat from every upright, unhaltered steed as well as the ball and spit of an everyman's dissident and delinquent cattle ... their bellowing, too ... not to mention their shit trail laid out in single file like flat-bottomed strudel showcased behind picture plate glass in some off-street bakery. I have been here before so many times that I know all of this and much, much more. Niitsííwa (It is true), itákkaa. Niitsííwa, my dear friend (itákkaa).

Today, it is my dream, and inside this day, my ipapaino, the talking dream ... the hour has arrived.

And, Big Brahma it is. "You and me, big man." That is what I say bravely. Me and Big Brahma. Two bull headed warriors together in one and the same holding pen. "For sure," I say out loud. Game on. Omatap, kemosahbee. Omatap. Iitsskáát! Or, to say in the white man's speech, "Begin the fight, brave warrior!"

Big Brahma, he is a big bull (áisaayoohkomi), and, he is quick. Ikkamssi. In spite of his size, the other riders, they tell me in private, he "Always twists right, lowers his head, and then prances before he turns back left" (like it will do any good). The turn (they say this, too) is with a vengeance similar to a hot, prairie cyclone in summer heat. You and your chaps and your sombrero, your quick thinking, and your rigging, these are your lone shelter. The other riders, they do not tell me this. This I just know.

Remember, I, too, am a rider and a good one.

This Big Brahma, he is rank and ornery and moody. Grumpy, too. Maksinámma. He is bad, maká'pssiwa, they tell me this. Some say he is too rank for his own good as the big man, he tries to kill each and every cowboy on the comeback with his crooked left horn or front him with the broad base of his thick skull. His two eyes bleed devil's fire. His stare is baleful but only to keep you inside his crosshairs so he can trample and gore you and come back to trample and gore you again a second, third, fourth, and fifth time until you are a lifeless rag doll, a dead man, an uprooted cadaver in the center of all this, his arena. It is all in fun. It is purely for show. He is master. You are the pawn. All bull and no play, it is Big Brahma.

When I settle onto his broad back, my legs gripping, situating, and looking for a lock, I am thinking in full voice twists right, lowers his head; he will prance just before he turns back left while I am laying a flat braided second wrap into the palm of my gloved hand. I pull tight, then tighter still, then one last time until I tamp down harder on the third and fourth tug until I cannot feel my fist making it tighter than packed ice the way that I like it. Now, I know that I am ready and focused because I am numb.

I slap myself in the face twice on the right side (Indian rodeo ritual for good luck). Once more on the left (my mother, she is left handed, so once with the left hand for her; I know you will understand), then I nod. The chute opens, and Big Brahma jumps free and clear of the gate and full-strides into the center of the arena just like the showman that he is, wrenching this way and that, up and down and side to side. The bell is clanking underneath, the crowd is roaring, and I am hanging on for dear life. I do not have time to breathe much less curse. If you have not been here, it is akin to riding the biggest bomb in the belly of the Enola Gay. Afraid? Iko'po? Only a fool would not be afraid, and I am not a fool.

Time can surely stand still for I am sure that I have seen it, just as now and in this moment. This way, then that way and back, we are in rhythm. My legs and spurs are dug in harder than Christmas frost. Eight seconds is a lifetime, but what do I care? I am still atop Big Brahma. The bull and my riding hand are still cinched together, and I feel as limber as air. I see only bull horns, one crooked, as I am pushed forward in an unpleasant lunge and petulant lean into the swell that is his Brahma hump. It is a false and troubling pillow cushion of bone and muscle, free ride and semi-position. In the split-second meantime, I am reciting in the open air on the whip turn "Always he turns right, then lowers his head;" *I remember it today like it was then. But somewhere in here, the dream, it, too, twists left.*

Tonight, Big Brahma, he twists right. Yes. He does this. But, when I get to the part in my head that speaks to me and says, "then lowers his head", *Big Brahma changes course. He acts out. Like Satan, he changes the deck and the deal at once. Instead, of lowering his head (just my luck), he does the unthinkable, the unexpected. Big Brahma, he throws his head back. Then, he throws it back a second time. He catches me in the forehead and across the bridge of my nose, all of this at the same time. I see stars, a galaxy and the Milky Way. My nose is split down the middle, my left eye and forehead, too. My face is busted and scrambled at angles parallel to one another and those same stars and some other galaxy. It is pressed and battered flesh, and blood ... my blood, nitsáápani, is slinging all about in the open air like spring rain on top of a red gusher. Still worse, I am tossed from mount to a sordid, sloppy, and dishonorable dismount and left dangling by one hand like a neckless horse thief on the wrong end of a hangman's noose. All of this would have hurt and caused pain, but I am out on my feet, or off my feet as it is, and unstarched and tossed about, to and fro, around the arena in a breached and sideways roil.*

I am a scarecrow afloat in a winter chinook.

The dream is still in force. But, here, it changes again ... just that quickly without cause or hesitation, rhyme or reason.

Now, Habib (yes, prison Habib), he, too, is here in Belle Fourche. He, too, is at these very same fairgrounds, and he, too, is inside the rodeo arena with Big Brahma and me, Hiram Johnny Walker Quicksilver, the rodeo bull rider. This is what my dreams tells me, much of it in Siksiká, the rest in cowboy rodeo English. I can understand it all, every word, in whatever translation. To dream in your native tongue, it is the mark of a true Indian. Mark it down, itákkaa! So says the dream mockingly but with native pride.

Habib appears from out of nowhere. He does not speak but steps forward into this same dream and slowly walks to the center of the arena. He is dressed in a religious gown. It is gauzy and loose and falls well below his knees nearly to the ground like the undercarriage of a caterpillar. His presence is somehow ominous like it could be filled with dread, but the dream does not tell me anymore than what I have just told you. In another closer look, this getup that Habib is wearing appears to be some kind of small, leftover tent, say from a travelling circus, like a portable barker's bin which makes it so that he can barely find an open hole in all the garment as he reaches out tentatively to raise his own two arms. His neck is buried under a long piece of cloth, a desert scarf. His head is covered in another swath of similar, colorless fabric too pale to describe, too wispy for a disguise.

He places his two hands into the thin, cool, evening air, and Moses-like, parts the great bull from his anger, his unsettled froth and fury and his vile temperament. These two, they stand before one another like blood brothers, two warriors. They are two, splendid victors for neither has lost. They meet at eye level. They stare and breath in staggered cadence, in muffled but earthy and jaundiced tones, each one too fearlessly baffled and stymied by the other to warrant the other's rebuff.

The bull, Big Brahma, he is quieted. The crowd, too. Now, the center stage is a shaman, a black and brutish áísaayoohkmoi (bull), and an Indian cowboy with a bludgeoned, unknowable face sprawled out on the dirt floor with an arm still fettered somehow to the giant beast that is now still and without movement.

This is all so sudden, yet it is to my delight. The crowd is hushed.

The bull breathes. His nostrils flair. He stands proudly (his nature). He is at rest. For certain, this is a miracle of someone else's religion, and I am spared. Praise the Great Spirit in the sky, Á'pistotooki, and Jesus, too. Salvation to impart. Habib and Big Brahma, they remain in look-off.

And, as for me? I am still hanging there regaining consciousness. My chaps lay cross-legged. My contestant number, it is upside down and flagging in a still breeze.

Contestant number 822 ... It is the last thing that I see in this part of my dream. Contestant number 822. It is in red. In block numerals. On a single sheet of fibrous paper pinned under the back yolk of my pearl snap rodeo shirt. 822, for sure. I can see it clearly, unmistakably even upside down and as contorted as I am. But, my shirt, my best cowboy rodeo shirt, it is ruined, shredded and bloodstained.

Seconds later, I am older, but, again, I am in Belle Fourche. This time, I am propped up on a battered left elbow sitting on my dirty backside with both knees folded up in front of me; my two feet, boots and spurs, they are casually planted, but I am comfortable on the ground. I even reach out to spin my left rowel with an index finger three times just to watch it spin. I can feel the added years at the back of my boot heels, even in my stance and the crease behind both of my knees as I try to straighten up. My knees, they are flimsy like crepe paper and suspect like flour and water mixed but not yet dry to the touch. Somehow, I am erect if only unsure and unsteady.

I must look a sight here all alone. I have been cut away from the back of Big Brahma before he is led away quietly, docile-like, on a loose halter and white lead rope by a small Blackfeet Indian girl wearing a braided ponytail, a soft, doe skin dress and moccasins beaded in bright turquoise and lined with a shiny pelt. The arena stadium, its bleachers and grandstand, its cattle chutes and trailer spaces, they are all empty now. The spectators have all gone. The dome lights are switched off, and moonglow is all that is left in the cast. Even so, it is bright and luminescent and plenty to see by.

I can feel the dark, cool dirt of the arena beneath me because it is lumpy, already stale and dry with clods the size of bull frogs that have been trampled out into the open from animal hoofs beating out their own direction in some earlier cavalcade or cowboy go-round. But now, it is useless. The same ground, it will be still and forsaken and weather-beaten for another year to come like nothing had ever happened here.

When I awaken, the two guards, they are smiling, looking down at me.

"Hiram Johnny Walker Quicksilver." That is what the one says, the taller of the two.

"Yes," I say in return, "That is me."

"Time to go home, kemosahbee," he says to me the Indian. "Pack your belongings. We will see you to the front gate."

It was a good day. This day I became a free man again. Yes, it was a very good day indeed.

It is no wonder that I remember this dream… for sure.

Chapter 28

Áókaki'tsi
Scouting Ahead

*W*hen we go to Isabella's Garden (the museum) to check it out, it is just me and Jesus. (Nice place. Not like I had expected, but still a nice place.) Me and Jesus, we travelled alone. We split up to cover our tracks. I went in the subway car. I think Jesus took a taxi. Don't know. Didn't ask. Told him not to hitchhike. (Hitchhike: a little Blackfoot warrior humor for you, again. Talking Jesus here, kemosahbee.)

Anyway.

Remember, we are on the secret mission.

I got on beneath the dirty street. The doors opened when the train stopped. I stepped in, and away we went. It was the fifth stop past where I got on. That's all I knew. I kept waiting and watching for the right get-off. Held onto the handle bars like the other people. No problem for a rodeo rider like me. Plus, go with the flow, so to speak. But, not just another Indian travelling on the underground locomotive, the secret iron horse, kemosahbee. This is the Quicksilver express carrying the Blackfoot Indian warrior, áwaawahkao'tsii, Hiram Johnny Walker Quicksilver, in a sneak attack against the enemy, Custer's ancestors, like at Fort Apache, John Wayne's Fort Apache. Aka, Isabella Stewart's

Garden & Museum. Take her paintings (not to mention the money) the way she took our land. Today, I am not even wearing the war paint, no tomahawk, no bow and arrows, no moccasins either. Just the big ass zapatillas Jesus told me to bring with the underground rail ticket stuffed into and sticking out from under the pearl snap button of my Western shirt pocket. It is my best rodeo shirt, the one with the black piping and the Pro Rodeo stamp on the cuff.

("Underground locomotive and the secret iron horse" ... those are another couple of good ones I thought you might like. For you, from me, the rodeo brave. Quick knows funny.)

Anyway. The car almost emptied there. I thought 'this must be where everyone goes to the museum,' but that wasn't the case.

Up on the street level, most of the people had already disappeared into the traffic and the nearby buildings. Then, it was just me again.

I saw Jesus from a distance. He saw me, too, but we didn't wave or say nothing to each other. Remember, we are on the secret mission. We acted like professionals, spies maybe, you know, like we didn't know each other, undercover so to speak. Jesus was even better at it than me, but I am friendlier than Jesus.

I went in first and looked around, stood over by the first room of pictures where the girls and boys were gathered. Some old women (kipitáaakií), too. There was gray hair and spectacles all around. Jesus, he came in past the no smoking signs a few minutes later. You know, like we weren't together. Like we'd never seen each other. I motioned to him from off to the side and walked into the second room, you know, like he knew what he was doing and what he was looking for, and like I knew what I was doing and what I was looking for.

Any time I need to bluff my way through a mare's nest, I stand straight up like my back is against the wall, Chief Totem Pole, with my arms folded, use the Indian scowl as cover looking up and down at the same time over the breadth of my high cheekbones with the corners of mouth turned downward and south, you know, toward my big ass Injun feet. Always works. No one fucks with ... yisstissitoto, Blackfeet for 'nobody fucks with' ... Hiram Johnny Walker Quicksilver ... not looking the way that I look.

Like I said, Jesus, he had been looking at books and memorizing art shit so in a way he was interested. More in the money, for sure, but a little in the paintings.

One group of girls and boys stood around like little statues. A woman spoke softly giving them a heads-up on what they were looking at, the paintings and stuff. I listened. Figured I might learn something about what I was getting ready to steal, so why not. No price tags. Wasn't like that. More say horse flesh at an open sale in a peculiar town with an auctioneer that stutters. Don't know what you're getting till you get it home and let it out of the barn. Buyer's luck. Right now, I am just looking the gift horse in the mouth.

CHAPTER 29

Stand Up at the Comedy Lair
Featuring
Hobby Alif Ali-Ali

The Persian Laugh Master _ Iran's Own Henny
Youngman Fatwa from a Funny Man

All of this was penciled in on a stationary sidewalk sandwich board in a chalk color mix of tangerine and lemon chiffon. The two pieces were propped up in a crooked lean-to just outside the canopied entrance to the nightclub's front door.

His Comedy Lair monologue began like this. (He was still trying to catch his breath when he got to the stage.)

"Testicles, one, two, three." Habib tapped the head of the microphone, politely.   "Testicles one, two, three." He then smiled. A star is born.

Habib Alif Ali-Ali had parked the cab outside in a No Parking Zone next to a very yellow fire hydrant. The taxi's orange, emergency four-way flashers that he left burning beat out a singular pulse or drumbeat like some kind of static dénouement signaling ... *chill, meter maids and patrol cars, I, Hobby Alif Ali-Ali, the comedy king, the mullah of madcap, will return very soon to move the car, my taxi. I am here to pick up Fame and Fortune, the two twin siblings who called in needing a lift.*

His cabbie i.d. hung from the rearview mirror, that instead of the fuzzy dice that hung from the rearview mirror of his girlfriend's mostly late model coupé. Cabbie No. 068721. His photo (a bleak likeness) and cabbie medallion came shielded in a clear plastic sleeve with a taxi yellow border. The taxi dispatch receiver blurted pickup and delivery info at random to an empty space and the universe beyond. You could hear bits and pieces of it from the outside through the crack at the top the taxi window. In Habib's mind, it represented a show of force. All the activity, the motion, the voices, the lights, the blurbs, they signified all things *cabbie* as well as the responsible and hustling taxi driver's quick and impending return. I am inside, it said, and soon, I will responsibly return to my other job. I am Habib Alif Ali-Ali, the Fatwa's Funny Man. So, chill.

He'd flicked the meter to off when he stuffed the key (yellow tagged) into his trouser pocket.

This was who he really was.

This was who he was really meant to be.

He spoke openly into a statuesque microphone that he caressed like a long, slender lover ... her legs up to here and as tightly wound as a riding crop. She was as sensuous, salacious, and sumptuous as Habib was ready for business, his own walk of fame, and a vagrant spotlight ready to show off his finely honed one liners and adept punch lines. His wares. He was no less the wordsmith from the steaming sands of the sub-Sahara.

"Two Arabs in full dress go into a bar. Both men sit at the bar and the one Arab says, Ya hazaa, Mister Bartender, I'll have a vodka martini straight up with a Greek olive. No, make that two Greek olives."

Habib felt he was on a roll. He smiled almost lasciviously at the scattered gathering. A two top here. A three top there. Twenty people maybe thirty altogether counting the bartender, two cocktail waitresses, a smallish bouncer (it's comedy), the manager, three busboys, a single dishwasher, and the sound guy, Deaf Leopard (again, it's comedy).

"The other Arab, he just watches," said Habib, pausing, continuing, gesturing dismissively with his free hand, "Does not say anything. After a minute or two, the bartender looks the way of the other Arab and asks, How about you? You drinking tonight? To which the other Arab replies, I'll have a camel's milk straight up and a Christian woman to go."

He grins (as if out loud) and waits on the laughter, the applause, the delivery recognition. There is nothing.

"Now," said Habib in a tutorial retort, "That's one funny thing after another that is what that joke is. Now, what I say, Ray Charles, yourself," said Habib into the dead space left before him. "I want to thank you for having me and thank you for coming out tonight. May Allah bless America. And may Allah bless all the women of America, for America's women they are so fine. What I say, again, Ray Charles? Huh? And, Pretty woman, this Roy Orbison ... he and his father knows best, too."

He was (though sparsely or barely followed if at all and only on Tuesdays and Thursdays) The Persian Laugh Master, Islam's Answer to Henny Youngman, Hobby Does Henny, The Emirate Laugh Master, A Funny Man's Fatwa, Mecca's Mime, A Fatwa in Funnyville, Fatwa Does Funny, Jihad on the Half Shell, & Laughing All the Way to Virginville _ Allah Approved, though nothing had caught on.

This was Tuesday nights.

Thursday nights, his routine went like this.

"Testicles, one, two, three," he began again, and, again, he tapped politely on the mic's mesh the same way as Tuesday night. He practiced at home with a broom handle embedded into the handle of a boom box. Thursdays were an experiment. Explore and conquer. Tear down the East-West walls of improvisation. Tuesdays the regular, established routine when he anticipated the big laughs, the really, really big laughs, then the standing ovation near the end before the curtain call, during the curtain call, and after the final curtain call, an *aw-shucks* return for one more round of self-deprecating recognition, and the cacophonous crescendo.

It never came.

Habib continued.

"Today, I pick up this man. He was coming to the airport to downtown. He says to me, Cabbie ... he does not know my real name is Habib even though it is posted on the dashboard with my photograph. The photograph is even darker than I am, so it is dark. I am brown, for sure, but my dashboard photograph is the color of Hershey's with almonds my favorite candy bar and my American girlfriend's favorite candy bar, too.

I feel so American sometimes I want to break out into the Star-Spangled Banner. But, then, I think ... Habib, you are a transplant from Iran. Do not sing the Star-Spangled Banner because you might get arrested. Not only that, you do not know the words. Not yet anyway. I am working on it. Okay? Jesus H. Christ. You know, the other guy. So, I don't sing out loud, only in the cab when I am alone and, then usually something in Arabic, an Islamic chant maybe, something more familiar in my native tongue.

So, anyway, this man he says Cabbie, what is happening in your town tonight, dude? Where are the girls? The beautiful girls? The ones that would like to be with a gentleman such as myself this very evening?

I love this. Only in America can the man arrive in the strange city and demand to go to the place where the dozens or more beautiful women will be. It is most surely the reason I am learning the words to the Star-Spangled Banner. For the women of America, one and all, it is for you.

Tuesdays and Thursdays Habib filled in at The Comedy Lair (Up & Comers, Latent & Late Bloomers Open Mic Night) on 34th and Tunnel Avenue. This was Tuesday. His schtick was a head wrap, tattered sandals for effect, with dark socks for warmth; it's New England. The accent was real. It was distinct. It was dripping of his homeland, Arabic contorted in a half twist and double front forward dismount to American English, without a hint of apology to the listener because he was oblivious to his own linguistic alter-cadence and redacted syntax. He was Habib, the comic.

He was after all a free man. He now lived in the West. He had a Western girlfriend. He had fooled everyone so far as to his mission, the jihadist thing, for his real desire, besides the American chick, was comedy. He was too awkward, too self infused, too culturally clumsy, too guileless and unsuspecting and inexperienced to know that he *wasn't dying up there* ... hot mic and all.

Still, no one in club Comedy Lair laughed. Everyone was simply bewildered by the man in the head wrap, dark socks and worn sandals who is covered in baggie pants and a button-down collared oxford shirt. When Habib finally left the stage, he drew a staggered, aseptic applause ... more relief than courtesy. Habib thought this a good omen. The next big thing I am, no doubt, he concluded.

He was back on Thursday before eight mixing and shaping his facial expressions in front of the tiny mirror under the demi drape of an open dressing cubicle. He wriggled straight his embroidered keffiyeh and saddled next to him in one hand his carryon Koran, in the other a strand of blue-eyed nazar love beads, a good luck charm from Myrna.

Habib's comedy routine Part ll, Thursdays, Final Take __

"People here thinks they are so intellectual ... so smart for sure. All the American people love to quote Einstein. They want to talk about the relativity theory. Okay, I say. So, I say, I will read it, Mister Einstein's book. So, I do. I read it. It is in Arabic, too, you know. Boring. That's what I say. Maybe it is better in English, but I doubt this very much and seriously. Nothing could be so uninteresting in any language is what I say. But, also, nowhere in the book did I see one mention of anyone in my family. No aunts. No uncles. No cousins. Not one relative. No names in there of anyone with which I am familiar. So, I say, Habib, what good is it if I refer to this Mister Smarty Pants Einstein? He knows everything but not one name of one of my relatives. How is it that this man is the smartest man ever to live?"

He waited on the laughter and the applause. He bowed. He straightened himself and smiled as broadly as any Rajput Scripps spelling bee champion at sendoff. Imperially, he bowed again and straightened himself again to that same smile. Somehow for Habib, it was as though it could have gone on forever.

Imperviously, he offered up the V sign, the peace sign, the number two & second to none sign, the political V for victory sign … offered it up left, right, and down the middle as well as to those way at the back of the room; it was all as one. Silence prevailed even over the chatter in the far rear corner. (A need-a-drink heckler at the service attendant station eyeing the waitress in short, short sleeves and an even tighter sweater.)

Habib Alif Ali-Ali skipped off, stage left, flagged another V over his right shoulder, and hurried out the back door. His Yellow Cab, No. 068721, was parked in one of the employee spots. He hopped in, started the car, and took a radio call for another pickup. Just another day in the life of a budding comedic savant.

But wait, said a voice. There's a note.

There was an envelope scotch taped across the front of his taxi meter, and a yellow stick 'em attached, handwritten that said, Read This! *Very Important* in bold letters.

He uncovered the letter and unfolded the paper inside, then read aloud:

Mission 2. We move at dawn. Be fully armed and in position to strike by 5 A.M. We will be there watching you. You are first. Head to the front of the building. Ring the bell. When the guard answers, self-detonate. Allah will be guarding over you, Habib. Seventy-seven virgins await you. I have requested another dozen for good measure. Allah has promised He will make it happen. Be brave, oh great jihadist. Be brave. Your comrade and leader, Imani Kahn.

CHAPTER 30

Eighty-One Minutes
At
Isabella Stewart's Garden
(The Museum)

Sometimes Jesus is smarter than you think. Sometimes I, Hiram Johnny Walker Quicksilver, am smarter than I think, too. And, okaki ... It is good to know wise choices.

We were supposed to meet City Chief and his meskwaki, the girlfriend, later at the other motel on the other side of town. It was closer to the museum we intended to rob. We were supposed to go over the plan for later that night. The plan called for the heist on Monday. March 19th. It was very early (or late night) Sunday, March 18th. Indian time... say, twelve something, quarter to one. Close enough.

Jesus, he's smoking reefer and contemplating. TV's going. Old movie. Sound's off or you can barely hear it. Gary Cooper is loping a pinto. He is all dressed in fancy buckskin. And, a good-looking horse, for sure. The pinto's breath is burning from his nostrils like white steam from a rail car's boiler dome on a clear day. Yaahssi (pleasing to look at) is Gary Cooper. He is the cowboy; the cowboy's cowboy, too. Tall in the saddle, a broad brimmed hat and fringe long enough to braid dangling from his waist jacket like he was one of us.

Jesus, he's thinking real hard about now. I can tell. And, then, all of a sudden, he jumps up and looks hard across the motel room at me and says, "Screw 'em," (says it in Spanish, "Atornillar ambos," just like that). But, I knew what he meant. He said, "We'll go now, tonight, kemosahbee. Noche. We'll take the stuff for ourselves and be gone. Por la mañana. No los necesitamos."

I didn't say nothing. I just smiled. Sometimes, you know you know, and you just don't need to say nothing when you know.

Heigh Ho. Heigh Ho. I think this to myself because I am happy in our plan.

We, me and Jesus, we came out of the motel room at a quarter past the hour. Pretty funny seeing Jesús Ángel Escobar with his hair slicked back, his shoes shined, clean shaven, all dressed up in a blue cop's uniform, his cap under his arm formal-like, the same cop uniform City Chief had rented us from Quite Contrary Mary's Crosstown Cross Dress, Dress-up, and Halloween. Jesus, he was a sight for sore eyes (just not mine). A mix of bellhop and Canadian military.

I looked pretty dapper, too. Injun cleans up good. Shoes spit shined (USMC). Brass polished. Everything including the gun and holster. So, we pile into Esther's sister's Cadillac.

There are only a few cars on the street. We make it to the location in little or no time and faster than we think. There was the side entrance. We parked. We walked up to the door.

Jesus says, "Ring the bell, bro'." So, I rang the bell.

I told Jesus, "Let me do the talking." (I'm thinking the accent. Too much Spanish for late night, pitch black, and big city museum all in one.)

The voice inside said, "Can I help you?"

I said, "Police." (Sounded like I meant business). "We have a report of a disturbance. Just wanted to check things out."

The voice from inside said, "Okay. I'll hit the button. Enter through the side door. You can come on in and take a look around."

Just like that, me and Jesus are inside and setting up shop. Piece of cake. Pedazo de pastel, for sure, replied Jesus.

Fred came out first from around the corner. He was average size, museum security uniform, in need of a haircut and a shave, but I don't say nothing. Says his partner is in the other room snoozing. Me and Jesus, we say stick 'em up, just like that. Jesus already has his gun out in the open. He's waving it about.

Fred surrendered, said, "Don't hurt me and take what you want."

"Seguro," said Jesus. "No hay problema."

Barney came around the corner, yawning. Wakes up when he saw us holding two pistols with Fred tied up in the chair behind us. Put his hands up in the air. Jesus motioned him to sit beside Fred. We tied him up just like Fred. Matching tie ups. Kind of cute. The gag is an old sock, clean, but an old sock, prison issue. Like I said, it was clean. The guards, they ain't done nothing. Just drawing a paycheck. Then, we, me and Jesus, come along out of the blue. So, yeah, the sock, it was clean.

The first room was big, tall, tall ceilings, higher than a cougar's ledge on a rocky trail. The walls were full of pictures in frames and artwork, decorative stuff all around. Jesus had the to-do list in his coat pocket. He pulled it out and began to point, this way and that. Take that one, he points. So, I take that one. And that one, he points out in the pale light. So, I take that one, too. This was like poaching cattle but easier and not as messy. The pictures ain't bellowing back at you in the moonlight. A snip here and a snip there and they're ready to load.

The press clippings said we was in there eighty-one minutes, but it was less than that. By the clock on the dashboard of Esther's sister's Cadillac (Indian time), I figured we spent an hour at best, maybe less. Then we were gone. Adios Isabella's museum. And... Ona'pssi (Indian for haul ass) ... from the Blackfoot warrior. It was that quick. Never said goodbye to Fred and Barney, but they were tied up comfortable enough until someone could get to them in the a.m. No hard feelings, náápiikoan itákkaa (white friends). Injun's gotta eat; baby horses need new shoes.

CHAPTER 31

A Day Late

It was early morning on the nineteenth. And, yes, it is March noted Habib. He'd been awake since before dawn.

His ship hadn't come in. He thought that it would have been there by now, but it hadn't. Nothing. Days, months, years had gone by. Still nothing. Looking out over the flat horizon, the stillness of the dawn's water, there wasn't a gull or a tern or tell-tale cloud much less the mast or pointy bow of some ship as premonition of good fortune to come. All things measured and stacked in a row, it really didn't look like it was going to happen. Not in this life anyway. So, he made the walk three blocks away from the wharf to the business district.

The street corner was quite busy. It bustled with cars and pedestrians, street cops and standbys, buses and taxi cabs all in single file along and across the lighted crosswalk.

Habib thought to himself:

Deep down, what is the real, quintessential difference between the religious zealot and the stupid man? Commitment and foolhardiness? The devoted man and the dolt? And, too, where is the dividing line between allegiance and abject denial? As well, the compartmental claim between rational choice and circumspect, obtuse coercion?

Then, he paused. Without taking a step, the answer came to him inside his head in a clear, mellifluent voice. The answer spoke up clearly:

Habib, there is a world of difference. Don't be a fool. Get a grip on yourself, my brother, before it's too late!

And, inquired Habib-the-inner-voice, *is this kamikaze stuff really translated literally and properly, not to mention suitably in context and in cinque with today's modern Quran?*

He thought not.

But, he thought almost aloud, *I am committed. I have pledged myself to Allah. Fatwa is fatwa. The die is cast. Jihad is the order of the day, soup de jour, and today's blue light special in one.*

He adjusted the wedge of plastic explosive crisscrossing his crotch (his left testicle was pinned left under the hard shell. It pained him in particular.) and pinching the nubby tip of his penis. It, too, was most uncomfortable. Seems I've been here before, he thought sarcastically scolding himself.

He looked up. He looked around; his predicament was written all over his Arab face. The crosswalk light signaled green again, but Habib stood frozen. Walking with the coil of detonatable putty in and around and between his balls and his thighs and his dick and his potbelly and his flaccid nipples and his sweaty armpits, serpentine and vine-like in the same bite ... for Habib, it was pure misery. To die in such self-inflicted discomfort seemed utterly senseless, misplaced, and unpurposeful. But who was he to question the interteaching, the directional, and decision as preordained triumph of the great and masterful Mullah of cell 69 straight off Air Islam flight 666 and last week's jihadistic, five thousand member convention in Nairobi. (So he said.)

Fatwa, fatwa, fatwa, said his inner voice. Or, was that fuck this, fuck this, fuck this as translated by some other inner self.

He fidgeted again with the bandolier wrap across his chest hidden beneath the drape of the unstarched dashiki jumpsuit.

You are here, the voice said inwardly aloud.

He saw himself in that moment in an out of body experience of sorts. A stone, wild eyed gargoyle upright from its crouch and pedestal, toothless, fangless yet absorbedly observant and cool. At the same time, he was looking down from aloft as if airborne much like some lighted fixture on a subway terminal where X marks the spot from which you are standing and intending to commence your journey. Looking straight down at the concrete beneath his feet, then all round at street level and the street corner and the passersby all flickering and aflutter hurriedly rushing hither and yon, they all seemed to be innocents at his mercy. As he Habib just stood there, frozen in a new-found self-pity, vacuously looking down at his feet one minute then back up and across the way at traffic lights and cars and buses and sooty fumes and a woman in a gray scarf and a man with bushy hair and two children too young it seemed for the rest of the crowd, all this at the corner of 23rd and Salem. The difference, as seemed to be spelled out in no nonsense American know-how, was literally life and death and there was just such fuzzy, unrelated, and intangible consequence in the concept of death itself. *Fuck this*, said Habib clearly to himself in an American-accented, anti-American rant. He fumbled for a second or two beneath the cloth covering his belly and unstrapped the lead wire to the detonator. He inhaled most deeply, then exhaled just as profoundly to twice as poignantly and profoundly exhale again in double time. Jesus, muttered Habib and pardon the pun, he told himself. Thank God that's over.

Habib packed his duffel-briefcase over his shoulder and made his way down into the subway terminal. He stood alongside the rails and waited for the D train. It was minutes from arrival. He peered deep into the dark recesses of the tunnel waiting on the single beam of light to pierce the darkness beyond. He heard the clatter and then no sooner the cars passed one by one until the carrier had stopped, the doors in front of him opened, and he could board. He was off to Ruggles street. Jihad was predestined. He was Jihad. The

Christian artwork was doomed, of this he was sure. He knew his fellow believers were among him. He could feel their prayers of guidance and best wishes. Of this, he was certain. *I love you, Myrna,* he whispered holding the subway strap above his head. Allah will care for you. It is destiny and the will of the divine.

He offed at Ruggles Street Station and waddled, bomb-strapped, to the top of the staircase into the open air. He could see the Gardner from where he now stood.

Peculiarly, it appeared the area was cluttered with activity. Yellow tape cordoned off a wide swath just before the Museum entrance. Police stood all around. Squad cars sat still with lights aglow, blue and strobe-lite. Metro squeakers voiced commands through the chill of the open air. It was more a battle zone than a tourist spot. He looked harder.

"What's happened?" said one bystander to another.

"The museum was robbed," said the one.

"Oh, my," said the bystander. "I was looking so forward to visiting the museum today."

"Not today, I'm afraid," said the other.

"Oh, well," said the bystander. "I'll come again." Before walking away, he asked, "Do they know who did it?"

"No," said the other. "Not a clue."

Habib stood for moment drinking from this fountain of new information just handed him by the conversation of these two strangers. He was puzzled and frustrated at first. His mission had been unceremoniously aborted. But, then as quickly it dawned on him, *I am free from death!* In a blink, his celebration had begun.

I can now return to Myrna and share the good news with her. She will be so happy to know that Allah has spared me. It was not His will for me to die this day and in this place. There are greater things in store.

He skipped backwards twice, turned on his left foot, and sat down on a park bench to unstrap the explosives from inside his robe. He unraveled them one by one and stuffed them into a park trash bin. He unseated the plastic trash liner from the metal stand and tossed it over this shoulder and made hastily back to Ruggles Street and down the subway stairway to the terminal ramp. There, he waited again for Train D, the Orange Line, this time headed the opposite direction toward home. He was joyous, gleeful, and inspired (he knew by Allah) and all of this at the same time and in a muddled instant.

Myrna will not believe her eyes when I appear in the doorway of our apartment. That is what he thought, and it made him smile.

From the subway terminal, Habib walked a half block to the spot where he'd parked his taxi, climbed in, and drove the seven blocks back to the apartment. He couldn't wait to tell Myrna the good news.

Habib climbed the stairway to his apartment. He felt a new-found spring in his step like he was riding on air. This was his magic carpet to Myrna, he thought. He smiled even broader as he pressed the key into the front door and swung open the door ready to surprise his one true love.

"Myrna," he said softly.

But there was no answer.

"Myrna," he said again.

From the next room, he could hear the sound of two voices. He was curious at first but just as quickly he became concerned. What is this? He thought. What are these sounds.

He moved toward the door of their bedroom, pushed open the door, and peeked into the room. There was Myrna naked, her back and buttocks unclothed, and she was panting. Her breasts faced away from the door where Habib stood toward her bed partner. Beneath her was another man whose dark silhouette looked familiar, but Habib was uncertain who the man was. He, Habib, was too overcome with horror and disbelief of her infidelity to react at first until instinct took over, and he blurted out,

"Myrna," said Habib. "What are you doing pray tell?"

As quickly Myrna replied, "What does it look like? I'm fucking Imani."

"Please," said the man-lover beneath her looking up. "How many times do I have to tell you, it's Wit ... Or, Witten. Witten Kingsland. As I have explained, Imani is merely my nom de guerre, dear girl."

She tossed her hair from her face to get a better view from over her shoulder. She then could see the man's silhouette standing in the open door, and a portion of his face became visible from the hallway light behind his right shoulder.

"Hobby, I thought you were dead?" said Myrna. "Why didn't you blow yourself up like Imani ... sorry ... like Wit said you were going to do?" Looking down at the man she sex-straddled, Myrna said, "Huh, Witten Kingsland?"

In the backdrop, the music was muffled but it could be vaguely distinguished.

Oh, baby, baby it's a wild world.

The threesome, only one clothed, stared vacantly at one another waiting to see how the unspoken, unbroken silence would end.

Trust in Allah, but tie up your camel _ old Arab proverb.

CHAPTER 32

Mohsokó ni Otomohk
The End of the Road

I could see Esther when I made the last turn past the stand of silver aspen and the giant, hollowed-out spruce. She was waiting on the porch stoop. Her chin was buried into the palms of her two hands. Her elbows rested on her knees just like they always did when she waited and she knew that I was coming home. I could see her smile even from the distance. Her brown skin, her pearly whites, her eyes aglow with anticipation ... it was Esther. I always saw her this way smiling and waiting for me just like she did when I went out hunting before daybreak and returned, just like she did when I went down the road, me, the rodeo cowboy, and returned, just like she did when I went off to prison and returned then, too. It still brings joy into my heart. Lust, too. I was so glad to finally be home and back on the reservation.

I never heard back from Jesus. On sunny days, and dark ones, too, I could still hear his voice inside my head. It was always his pirate mix of spoken words, Jesús Ángel Escobar's own malady, his bad seed, maka'pii, and the spirited moods, his devil-may-care madness broadcast in Jesus-real time with his mongrel-bandito delivery. Jesus, he was the crack at the end of the whip and gone almost as quickly as he had appeared. We was never good buddies, just prison mates.

Someone said he took his share of the art and put it up for sale. Said they saw it in a newspaper ad down in New Mexico. Fellow told me he got a few grand and moved on. Said he was homeless now. I was not surprised.

Someone else said he packed his part of the take around in a gunny sack like a hobo. Said he lived under a railroad trestle. Made a lean-to of cardboard and throw away wood scraps. Pulled out the artwork just to look at it when he drank tequila, then carefully and precisely wrapped it again just the way it was and stuffed it back inside the tote. The thrill for Jesus was always in the con, and, this time, it had worked.

Another somebody, a neighbor's neighbor that had only heard about Jesus, said he lived in an abandoned trailer. No windows, no doors. Nothing fancy to say the least. But, for him, the setup beat prison and his upbringing by a mile. The trailer was on a small patch of government land. No one took an interest, so no one noticed, so he made out. He was more like a hermit in a cave. Something to that effect. There was no mention of the paintings.

Another person told a friend of a friend that Jesus left his share of the heist in a warehouse and forgot about it. He drank mezcal for three days and three nights. Stayed stoned for another three after that. He'd hitched a ride with a señorita whose name he couldn't remember. A week went by, maybe longer, before he came to and finally sobered up, but even then, he couldn't remember nothing. He never found his way back down the mangy road to the place where he'd hid the loot. It was dark and starless the night he put it there. Between the hooch, the Mexican green, and pitch black, he had no sense of direction for the return.

Then, there was the sheriff's deputy from the next county over. Swore he heard it dispatched over citizens band. Breaker, breaker. Suspect, Ángel Escobar. (Funny to hear him (Jesus) called by his middle name.) Ex con. Art heist. Drug bust on a drug deal soured. In custody, it was reported. Said Jesus (Jesús), he was a Mexican. (The sheriff's deputy, he was positive it wasn't religious and quick to make that point clear.) Ten four, over. The ex con, he was picked up somewhere south of where he was but north of the border in broad daylight. So, the drug deal, it went all wrong. No drugs, no money, out the art, full circle. Hard to say for sure. We're talking Jesus here.

Maybe it was true what I heard. Don't know. Like I said, I never heard from Jesus. We was never good buddies, just prison mates. Never said we was art thiefs, but, we learned quick enough.

Me and Esther, we got three of the paintings set up in the big den in the trailer. They're over by the big screen TV. I liked Leaving the Paddock *(says so on the back) because it had horses in it, so Esther said why don't we put it highest up on the wall. So, we did. The other one, The Resurrection of Jesus ... supposed to be the most famous and worth the most money ... the Vatican loaner ... Jesus gave me the locker key just before we split. Said, "Aquí. For you, amigo. Locker número fifty nueve (59). The famous painting. Pintura famosa. What got this all started. Get to it before City Chief." So, I did. It's in the hallway leading to the master bedroom, you know where me and Esther make hay. There's a purple tomahawk hanging just above it that Esther won shooting plastic ducks in a big water barrel over at the Flathead County fair in Kalispell. Knocked over seven out of seven. It was Esther. Eight out of eight and she'd have won a life-size tom-tom covered in genuine elk hide. Would've been nice, but we both like the tomahawk about as much. The eagle feather sets it off for sure.*

No one much comes by to see us. Lily, her half-sister, and Geronimo Jerry, my old school pal. He drops by to drink a beer from time to time. We talk about rodeos coming up, both sanctioned and jackpots. Me and Geronimo, we both like the CFL, so we talk about that some, too. We'll watch **Price** *(Price is Right) mid mornings around ten thirty or eleven if he's around. Geronimo, he really knows his appliances. Cars and motorhomes, too; hell, I even believe he could win. But, no one really knows nothing about art so the pictures (the paintings) they go unnoticed. They could just as easily be velvet Elvises or Crazy Horse* *silk screens touting a lost Indian heritage. Who would know? And, really, how could anyone tell? Seems all the same.*

One day I'll pack all of it up and take it to a big auction somewhere. Missoula, Great Falls, say, maybe up to Calgary. You know, after all the hubbub dies down. Dress up like somebody else as a disguise. Then, me and Esther, we'll take a vacation with the extra money, maybe down to Tucson or Phoenix. Hitch up the camper. Maybe catch some Arizona steers for fun during the winter months when it's colder than Saskatchewan here and the snow's up above my truck tires. I'll take my roping saddle, my good blanket, the glittery spurs, and the rope sack (with my initials) just in case. Rodeo, it's just like riding a bike, you don't never forget.

But, who knows what will happen?

For now, me and Esther, we're here and settled in, two untamed, unbroke Indians chillin' in our double-wide teepee.

When the phone rang next, Esther answered then handed the phone over to Hiram and said, "It's for you." So, Hiram put down his beer and put the phone up next to his ear and said, "Hello," like you do … and then he heard that old, familiar voice say, "Hola, Quick! Cómo estás, amigo. Long time no see. Resucitó una vez más, amigo. Resurrected one more time, Quick! One more time for sure."

Nikááksista'pssi.

I have finished.

Ki Ánnimýai iihkakótsiiwa

This is where it concludes.

As Translated from Siksiká /Southern Piegan

Yancey Williams is a graduate of the University of Colorado. He lives in the low country of South Carolina.

For more information visit the author's website at:

www.yanceywilliams.com

Also by Yancey Williams:

Worlds Apart

Shoot the Messenger

Rome & Joliet

www.ingramcontent.com/pod-product-compliance
Lightning Source LLC
Chambersburg PA
CBHW021431110726
47901CB00008B/2377